POWER
OF
LIGHTNING

SUSAN McKENZIE

ReamStories subscription:
https://reamstories.com/susanmckenzie
Amazon author page:
https://www.amazon.com/author/susancarter
Visit Sue's website:
http://susanmckenzieauthor.com
Follow Sue on Facebook:
https://www.facebook.com/SueMcKenzieAuthor

YOUR FREE BOOK IS WAITING

The novelette

THE ALIEN

is free for a limited time. You just need to tell me where to send it

When Lilliana crash-lands her spaceship on a Primitive planet, she'll have to rely on help from an attractive local to survive.

Use the QR Code to follow the link, then enter your name and email address to get your free book delivered to your inbox

Or type this link into your browser: https://www.sub-

scribepage.com/thealien

WHAT READERS LIKE YOU ARE SAYING…

"The sweet little ghost won me over in the first book and didn't disappoint in the second. Her main villain was fabulously written because he made me hate him more and more with each appearance."
   – **angeljoei (Amazon review)**

"This second book was even better than the first. It has a little more action. A little romance and some intrigue. You've got the good, the bad and the Alien."
   – **Zippy Inger (Amazon review)**

"How I wish there were more than two books for this series! I loved the story and what they both overcame to be together."
   – **Travina (Amazon review)**

To my son, Shaun.

My greatest joy in life was becoming a mother. I'll always be here for you and I love you to the universe and back.

CHAPTER 1
Just Tell Us What Happened

I swiped my finger across the screen to access the next question.

HOW LONG HAVE YOU KNOWN ABOUT YOUR TALENT?

I frowned. I'd only managed to use my Talent to initiate a telepathic conversation for the first time a couple of days ago, so I typed in my answer.

OUR RECORDS INDICATE THAT YOU DID NOT DECLARE A RECOGNISED TALENT WHEN YOU APPLIED FOR THE POSITION OF NAVIGATIONAL COMPUTER OPERATOR WITH KATOA INTERGALACTIC MINING AND EXPLORATION. CAN YOU TELL US WHY YOU DID NOT DECLARE YOUR ABILITIES?

I didn't know I had any psychic abilities when I'd started working for the biggest mining company in the Known Universe five months ago.

"This is stupid," I said to no one.

The answer to the previous question kind of negated this one. How many more questions like this would I have to answer? This was getting ridiculous. The investigators from Katoa that were going to question me about the events surrounding the tunnel collapse down on the planet, Kronos, were probably going to ask me the same questions anyway.

I sighed and felt a twinge of pain from my broken ribs. I needed some more painkillers.

After a few more stupid questions, I wanted to throw the Palm-pad across the room.

A bright light had me shielding my eyes as my heartbeat picked up.

Once my eyes adjusted, I could make out the rough shape of a man made of coloured light floating before me.

I smiled.

"Allador!"

I was so relieved to see my alien friend, but worried that someone could walk in and cause a panic.

Allador inclined his head and answered me telepathically. *"Greetings, Lennina. It is good to see you."*

I wasn't sure what to say. "What are you doing up here on the station?"

"I wanted to heal you."

I sat with my mouth hanging open. He would risk being seen so he could heal my broken ribs?

"If that is acceptable to you?"

"Oh, um, yes... Thank you."

He moved forward slowly and reached out his hand. Once it made contact with my right side, warmth stretched out across my entire body. Closing my eyes, I relaxed and breathed a sigh of relief.

I trusted Allador after I'd seen him heal my work partner, Daniel Javolo, who'd had multiple injuries after the tunnel he was working in down on the planet had collapsed.

I felt one rib knit back together and it made me queasy. I'd felt the same thing when Allador had healed Daniel, through our weird connection that caused me to feel Daniel's pain, but this was different. This time I knew it was my bones.

The door swished open and a nurse walked in wheeling a cart. She screamed and Allador backed away from me.

"It's okay!" I told her. "He's not hurting me. He won't hurt you."

Her big brown eyes were wide and she was shaking. "What is that thing?"

How could I stop her from freaking out and calling security? "It's an alien from Kronos. His name is Allador."

"Wh-what's it doing here?"

"He was healing me."

She looked at me. "What?"

"He was healing my broken ribs." *And you interrupted.*

Allador fluttered around in the corner. *"I will return."*

Before I could say anything, he vanished.

"Where did it go?"

I crossed my arms. "He left because you were freaking out. He didn't get to finish healing me."

"Oh."

"Why are you here?"

"Oh, I came to give you a blood test. They said they told you about it."

I sighed. Might as well get it over with. "Yeah. So, where do you want me to sit?"

"Just on the edge of the bed. I'll position the cart to suit."

"Okay."

I sat and tried not to look as she took five vials of blood from my arm. That seemed like an excessive amount.

"Why so many vials?"

"Oh, there are so many things we need to test, and each one requires a different treatment of the sample."

"Oh." What else could I say to that? It wasn't like I could demand that she put it back.

After fiddling around with the vials and asking me to check my name and date of birth on the labels, she packed up her equipment and left me with a wish that I have a nice day. Considering who I'd be talking to next, I highly doubted it.

Sure enough, I didn't have to wait long for the two investigators to be ushered in to see me.

Dr Rowen said she'd leave us to it and left with a fake smile on her face, and the two well-dressed men stepped further into the room. They too, had fake smiles and I gave them one in return. I had nothing to smile about.

They introduced themselves as Mr Deunan and Mr Kessik, saying that I needn't worry as they just wanted to ask me some questions about what had happened on the day of the tunnel collapse. It was their job to interview everyone involved and try to piece together what had taken place and why, and blah, blah, blah.

I relaxed a little. They hadn't mentioned anything about a possible breach of regulations or any relationship with Daniel.

I knew I was still in a lot of trouble, though. Sonrisa had already blasted me for my slow reactions after it all happened, so I expected them to be asking about that too.

I waited and tried not to fidget. The first questions were pretty standard. How long had I worked for The Company and where was I from and so on. Then they asked about my first Digger, Arkena Rogan, which made me wonder why. Why would they ask about that? Did they think I had something to do with him seeing a "Ghost" in the tunnels and being taken off active duty to go to counselling?

And what did that have to do with the tunnel collapse?

Nothing.

The simple answer was: nothing. I took a deep breath. Maybe they were trying to intimidate me. It was possible. Or make it seem like I couldn't do my job properly. Both of my Diggers had "gone crazy," which is Katoa's explanation when anyone claims they've seen bright lights or a Ghost down on the planet. The Ghosts were real, though. They were Allador's people — a race of beings made out of light and energy.

The official word was that the planet was uninhabited. The Company couldn't let the people know that there was sentient life on the planet we were mining, because then they would have to get the inhabitants' permission to be able to continue mining.

I decided not to let them intimidate me. I had other, bigger things to worry about. I tried to answer the questions as best I could.

Then they finally decided to ask me about the events leading up to the collapse.

"Everything had been normal and the morning went ahead as usual," I said.

My mind kept wandering back to when I wanted to talk to Daniel and tell him how I felt about him, so I had to make sure I didn't say anything that would give any of that away. I just stuck to the facts surrounding the other events.

"Daniel had dumped a load of Amakio back at the shuttle and had finished digging out the next vein when he saw a bright light." There was no point in denying the Ghost sighting. It was all recorded.

When they looked at me questioningly, I sighed. "You would have heard what happened by listening to our recorded conversation."

"Never mind that," Kessik said calmly. "We want to hear your version of events."

I sighed again. "The recording *is* my version of events."

"Now, Miss Callista, there's no need for the sarcasm. Just tell us what happened."

I groaned. "That wasn't sarcasm..."

He exhaled heavily through his nose. "Just tell us what happened," he repeated.

I told them what I could remember, but as for the four minutes and twenty seven seconds before I made the first call, I didn't know what had happened to me. "I found myself on the floor, staring up at the ceiling. So I think that means I must have blacked out somehow." They didn't look convinced. "I've had several blackouts since then."

They simply nodded and Kessik typed something on his Palm-pad.

There was no hope of coming out of this unscathed, so I tried to be as truthful as possible. I'd have to leave some things out about Daniel and I.

They kept asking more and more questions and it reminded me of Malvolio when he was convinced I was already seeing Daniel and wouldn't even listen to me. It was upsetting to think about him. Those wounds were still raw. I'd forgotten about him for a while, even with the pain in my ribs to remind me every time I moved. I'd been so focused on Daniel. The memories flashed before me and the tears threatened to start. The pain in my chest flared and I couldn't think straight.

I tried to focus on the current situation, with no success.

"Why didn't you report to your supervisor right away that your Digger was in trouble?"

I tried to hold back my rising frustration. "I told you. I fainted. Play back the recording and you'll probably hear me fall to the floor. And you could probably hear me get back up again after the four minutes and whatever seconds..."

Kessik turned toward me. "Do you know the correct procedures to be followed in an emergency situation?"

I stared at him incredulously. "Yes, of course I do!"

He cocked a bushy eyebrow. "You seem to have had trouble carrying them out. Can you tell me why that is?"

"I told you..." I'd had enough. He was another Malvolio. I wanted them to go away and leave me alone. "Look, I'm not feeling—"

"What is the status of your relationship with Daniel Javolo?" Deunan interjected.

CHAPTER 2
A Pathetic Excuse for a Doctor

"What?" I wasn't expecting that question. I thought they were still stuck on the why-didn't-you-do-your-job track, so it caught me off-guard.

He sighed. "Do you have a relationship with Daniel Javolo?"

"No, I don't." It was kind of true. I couldn't call what we had a 'relationship.' It was a huge jumbled up mess, that's what it was. Maybe it could become a relationship, but that would have to wait till later. "There is no way I could have a relationship with a scratchy, off frequency voice on an outdated Com system."

"Oh, I don't know about that..."

I cringed inwardly. That sounded like a threat buried in there somewhere.

Stating the obvious facts wasn't working.

I was in trouble.

I remembered I'd quit my job. This was as good a time as any to tell these idiots. I took a deep breath. "I informed The Company on the day of the collapse that I wanted to resign my position."

That stopped them for a few seconds. It was something they clearly weren't expecting. But then, "What is company policy in regard to Navs and Diggers?"

I leaned forward, looking from one to the other. "Didn't you hear me? I've quit!"

"That is neither here nor there," Deunan informed me. "You were still employed by The Company at the time of the incident, and therefore are responsible for your actions, meaning that you are liable for any actions — or inactions — on your part."

"So," Kessik continued, "what is company policy when it comes to relationships between our Nav Operators and Diggers?"

I wanted to scream. "I know what they are!" I snapped. "But I told you already, there is no relationship! Just get out of here! I don't have to answer any more questions. I told you I quit!"

"And I told you it doesn't make any difference to this investigation," Deunan said.

How could I get them to listen?

"Your response times were too slow. This was an emergency situation. Your Digger's life was in your hands. He could have died because of your incompetence."

That was a stab to the heart. Tears stung my eyes. I tried to calm down, but it didn't help. "Get out! Leave me alone!"

Dr Rowen opened the door. "What's going on in here?" she asked.

Relief flooded me. "They won't leave," I told her. "I can't do this now and they won't stop asking questions."

"Now, gentlemen, you need to tone it down," she told them.

What?

"Okay, Doc," Deunan said.

He turned back to me and gave me that fake smile.

My ribs screamed as I turned to look at her. "Dr Rowen! What are you doing? I want them to leave!"

"They need to finish the interview," she said calmly.

I couldn't believe what I was hearing. What happened to telling me not to move around too much with the broken ribs?

"No — you don't understand. I'm not feeling well. I can't continue. Just get them out of here! Please!"

She said nothing.

Deunan continued on as if nothing had been said. "So, how long have you had this relationship with Daniel Javolo?"

"There is no relationship. We're work partners. We're not allowed to meet."

My blood was about to boil. How could the doctor stand there and let them do this?

Then it hit me. Dr Rowen was employed by Katoa. She didn't want to stop them from conducting their interview — it could affect her job here. She might lose her job or be transferred or something.

I headed for the door. "If you won't leave, then I will."

Both men grabbed me by the arms and marched me back to the bed, but I wouldn't sit back down. They pushed on my arms so hard their fingers dug into my flesh, so I was forced to sit.

I kept struggling to get free. "Let go of me!"

"Be gentle now, boys," Dr Rowen told them. Was that concern in her eyes? Probably not. It didn't matter. She wasn't going to stop them.

I yelled at them again. How could they do this to me?

I glared at Dr Rowen. A pathetic excuse for a doctor. *What is your problem? Stand up to them! You're supposed to help me here!*

"Get out! Get out!" I screamed. The pain in my ribs was getting worse. I wished Allador hadn't been interrupted.

One of the lights on the ceiling popped, and everyone flinched.

CHAPTER 3
We're Here to Help You

The door slid open and Dr Kharim came in, flanked by two burly men that looked like they were either wardsmen or security guards. "What's all the screaming about? What kind of interview is this?"

The two investigators started to talk, but I cut them off and told Dr Kharim what was going on, including the fact Dr Rowen hadn't stopped them or asked them to leave.

His frown deepened. In fact, his face went a lighter shade of brown. He started by telling Kessik and Deunan to leave, and the guards stepped forward to emphasize what he was saying. The scumbags gave me some scathing looks and took their leave, saying it wasn't over; I would hear from them again. I didn't care at that point, as long as they left.

As soon as they were out of the room, Dr Kharim's next move was to see if I was okay. Once I'd told him how much pain I was in, he said he'd organise some more pain relief. He made sure I was comfortable in the bed, then turned his attention to Dr Rowen.

He gave her a stern look, clearly trying to control his temper. "Dr Rowen. You know the patient is to remain still at all times. If you'd follow me so we can speak privately..."

I noticed the strain in his voice.

All the questions the investigators had asked raced through my mind as they left the room. Daniel and I were in for a bucket-load of trouble, but all I wanted to do was get out of here and see him. The pull toward him was so strong. I couldn't explain it. It couldn't be a normal thing when you're in love with someone. This weird feeling was beyond any natural connection or relationship with another person. Maybe it had something to do with the jolt of electricity we felt when we touched, and the awesome mind connection. I didn't know how or why it was there, but there was no denying it.

A nurse came in and gave me something for the pain.

I tried to make sense of all the things that had happened, but my mind was muddled, and as I lay on my back staring at the ceiling, I wondered what I was going to do next.

──── ★·☆·· ────

Once I'd had some lunch and was left alone again for about half an hour, Allador returned.

The sudden brightness hurt my eyes, but I was glad to see him.

"Greetings, Lennina."

"Hello, Allador."

"I have come to make sure you are fully healed. It will not do to have your injuries half-healed. It is not good for the body to stop before completion — even with my people, the Ampari."

Great. That's all I need. "Will there be permanent damage?"

"No. I will fix."

"Okay."

I sat still while he placed his hand on my side again and the warmth spread through me. It had a calming effect, and by the time he'd finished, I was sleepy.

"This is a normal reaction," Allador told me. *"You will feel sleepy for a while. This is good. I will take my leave now, before other humans enter this area."*

"Okay. Thank you so much." It was such a relief to be pain-free that I felt like crying.

He inclined his head. *"I will say farewell."*

"When will I see you—"

He disappeared.

What?

A nurse with jet-black hair pulled back in a severe bun entered the room and sat herself in a chair beside the bed, introducing herself as Simona.

I was glad Allador hadn't been discovered again. He must have known she was about to walk in.

She programmed a Bio-scan to scan my vitals.

"Just lie down and let it do its thing," she told me.

I watched as it floated above me, starting at my head and making its way down to my toes. My eyes were still recovering from Allador's bright light, so it was hard to focus on it. It travelled back up and landed on a shelf above my head when it was done.

"Why do you need to check my vitals? I thought I was in here so you could check my mind for Talent?"

"We need to do some tests to see why you've been passing out."

"Oh. I thought it was because I was using my Talent."

"Yes, but you shouldn't pass out every time."

"Okay. I didn't know. I don't really know anything about psychic abilities."

"You'll learn. We're here to help you."

I sighed. That was good to know. And once I got out of here, the Talent Training Centres (TTCs) back home would be able to help me with whatever training I would need.

And I needed to get out of here.

The investigators didn't talk about the breathable atmosphere on Kronos. They wouldn't want anyone to know about it, so I was determined to tell everyone I could before they slapped an order on Daniel and I to shut us up.

I decided to tell Simona. She could tell others and spread the word further. "Did you know there's air on Kronos?"

CHAPTER 4

I've Missed You

The nurse's eyes went wide. "What? No. Who told you that? It's toxic. It will kill you."

I sat up and looked her in the eye. "No. It won't. If you don't believe me, go and ask my Digger, Daniel Javolo. If it wasn't for the fact that there's a thin atmosphere on the planet, he would be dead right now."

I tried to keep my expression neutral, even as my words cut into my heart like a knife. I knew only too well how close he'd come to dying out there. I ignored the sting of tears. I didn't want to cry in front of this woman.

Simona casually typed some notes on her Palm-pad, then looked up at me. "Are you sure?"

"Yes, I'm sure. Go visit Daniel. He'll tell you everything. I could come with you and you can question us about it together. That way you could get all the information at the same time..."

Simona frowned. "No... I don't think so," she said slowly. "We have orders to keep you two apart."

My spirits sank. "Why?"

"They didn't tell us that bit."

Of course they didn't.

I was antsy. I couldn't explain why I felt an overwhelming urge to find Daniel and just wrap my arms around him... And kiss him again... warmth spread across my chest at that thought.

Simona asked a few more questions about my general health and gasped as she looked down at the Palm-pad again.

"What is it? What's wrong?"

"These readings can't be right."

"Why not?"

"It says you don't have broken ribs."

"I don't. Not anymore."

Her perfectly manicured eyebrows drew together. "What are you talking about?"

"The alien that healed Daniel? He was just here and he healed me too."

I lifted my shirt and showed her my still-glowing side.

Simona gasped again. "It was in here?" She looked around nervously, as if she expected him to appear at any moment. "I have to go tell the doctors."

She made a move to leave. "Oh, and there's a Mr Dermid waiting to see you."

I froze; my insides like ice. What was he doing here? What did he want?

"By himself?"

"Yes. Is there a problem?"

"Yes. He shouldn't be coming in here by himself. I have an RO out against him. They won't keep him away altogether, but I told them I didn't want to be alone with him. Just tell him to go away."

Simona's mouth dropped open. "You don't want to see him?"

Didn't you hear me? "Yes, that's right," I said. "I never want to see him again, but he's part of this whole thing with my Talent and that means I have to put up with him 'observing' things. So, like I said, tell him to go away."

Her eyes widened. "But Miss Callista. It's Malvolio Dermid! He is the MIC at Galaxy Mech. You can't tell him to just go away!"

I glared at her. "I can and I did..."

As I spoke, the door swished open.

There he was, holding a large bunch of flowers. Roses. Long-stemmed, red roses. His face moulded itself into a smile and he strode over to the bed, nodding to Simona. My heart pounded.

"Hello, Lennina, darling. It's so good to see you," he said warmly. "When I heard you were visited by one of those aliens, I was worried about you."

Memories of the night he broke my ribs flashed through my mind.

I clenched my fists. "I'm *not* your darling. You're not supposed to be near me without one of the doctors. I don't want to see you. I want you to leave."

Simona sucked in a breath.

Malvolio's smile stayed in place. "Now, Lennina, my love, there must be some misunderstanding. I've come to ask you to come back."

Simona fidgeted and got to her feet, clearly uncomfortable. "Well, I'll leave you two to talk things out..."

She headed to the door.

"Wait!" I called. "Don't go! He's not my boyfriend anymore and I don't want him back. He *assaulted* me."

Simona's face flushed red and a look of confusion spread across her features, but Malvolio assured her everything was fine. "She's just upset after all that's happened. She'll be okay."

I saw the way she looked at him. She actually liked him. Maybe she was infatuated. I wouldn't be getting any help from her.

Malvolio ushered Simona out the door while I tried to convince her to stay or get security, then he waved a hand to close the door and turned back to me and smiled. My heart sped up.

"Lennina. I've missed you."

I doubted it.

Being near him and hearing him say that seemed so much worse after spending time with Daniel and seeing how he genuinely cared about me. After feeling the warmth in his embrace. The desire in his kiss...

Malvolio stepped up to the side of the bed. "It's all arranged."

CHAPTER 5
It's That Heathen You Work With, Isn't It?

My chest tightened as I looked at the flowers and imagined him asking me to marry him. "What's all arranged?"

"You can start your new job once you've finished up here. You can be a part of the Research and Development team here at the station."

What? "But I'm going home to Azaeli once I've finished with all this crap."

He screwed up his face at the word *crap*. "What do you mean? This is the job you wanted. You said it would be your dream job."

"No. I didn't say that. I said it was the job I was planning to work towards. It wouldn't be my dream job."

My dream job would probably involve playing music.

He placed the flowers at the foot of the bed and started to pace. "I've organised it all for you, and now you're telling me you don't want it?"

"Yes. That's exactly what I'm saying. That's the job I wanted before you punched me in the face and kicked me in the ribs. I don't want to be here any longer than I have to. Once these tests and interviews are over, I'm outta here."

He stopped pacing. "You are so ungrateful. After all I've done—"

"I never asked you to organise it. I was perfectly happy to work my way up to the position on my own. But it doesn't matter now. I'm going home."

Malvolio's smile was infuriating. "But we were so *good* together."

"No. We weren't. I thought we were, but you ruined it."

He stepped closer. "I'm here because I am willing to forgive you."

"What? *You* are going to forgive *me?* For what?" I asked incredulously. "Ramming my ribs into your foot?"

He sat himself on the chair Simona had vacated. "Now, let's not go over it all again. I want you to come back and live with me this time. Then things will be better..."

"No! Never! I don't love you anymore. I can't forgive you for hurting me. I could *never* be with you after what you did."

He put a hand on my arm, but I quickly pulled it away. "Now, Lennina—"

"You don't get it, do you? You broke three of my ribs!"

He tried to look hurt. "Oh... no. I couldn't *possibly* have done that."

My heartbeat was erratic and I was having trouble breathing. "You *did!* Ask the medical staff for the x-rays!"

He shook his head, looking at no one in particular. "No. You must have had a fall... That's it... You fell here at work... You could claim compensation, you know..."

I couldn't believe it. He was doing it again. My breathing was shallow. I reached under the covers and found the button to buzz for the nurse and pressed it.

When I spoke, it seemed like it was in slow motion and I had to push each word out. "Will you stop it? *You* did it! You punched me in the face, then kicked me while I was lying on the floor!"

He seemed confused, like he was unable to comprehend what I was saying. Like he couldn't possibly have hurt me.

"What are you talking about?" He reached out a hand and touched my shoulder, but I shrugged him off.

"Nurse!" I shouted as I pressed the button again.

I heard movement outside, but no one entered.

He reached for me with both hands. "Don't push me away like that, Honey."

Honey?

He smiled as he stood up and leaned over me. "You need to calm down."

"Calm down? Don't tell me to calm down! And don't call me Honey! Nurse! Get him out of here!"

Those grey eyes turned darker. "It's that heathen you work with, isn't it?"

"He's not a heathen! Just get out!"

He leaned closer. "So I'm right. It *is* him. It's always been him. You've been *fucking* him all along, haven't you?"

I cringed. "No!"

He moved closer, his voice low and deadly. "Don't fucking lie to me. I knew you were up to something. I could see a change in you. There was something different about you. You were no longer *innocent*. That's when I knew you'd fucked him."

I was never 'innocent.' Not the way he was meaning. "No, I didn't. I didn't even know him..."

"But you know him now."

"I've met him now, yes."

"I *knew* it!" he said again. "You *were* fucking him! You *were* cheating on me!"

"No! I *wasn't!* I would never do that to someone!"

He raised a hand and I flinched, expecting him to hit me, but he gently stroked my hair. "Shhh. It's okay. I'm here."

What?

He grabbed me by the upper arms, digging his fingers into my flesh. I twisted to try to get away. "Let go! You're hurting me!"

"Shhh." He leaned forward to kiss me, but I turned my head away. That didn't stop him. He kissed me on the cheek instead, sending a chill through me. He was serious. He pushed me back slowly until I was lying on the bed, which scared the hell out of me.

I tried again to twist free. "Stop it!"

"Shhh. You need to just relax..."

Malvolio had to be crazy. He was delusional again. He leaned forward and kissed me, even though I was protesting and turning away from him.

I still had the buzzer in my hand so I held my finger on the button as I tried to cry out for help, tears streaming down my face. "Stop! Help! Someone help me!"

Why won't they help me? Why won't they stop him?

The flowers fell to the floor, forgotten. The buzzer was wrestled from my hands. "Come on, Honey. It's okay. I'm here now," he said between kisses. "I told you I'd show you what a real man feels like. I'll make you forget him."

Was he going to force himself on me right here in the bed?

"I'm *not* yours!" I screamed at him. "You don't *own* me! You can't just do whatever you want to me and expect me to not fight back!"

I struggled in vain as he grabbed my face between his hands and kissed me on the lips. I was trying to hit him and kick him, but it didn't stop him. He was trying to part my lips and deepen the kiss, and I was struggling to keep my mouth closed.

The door finally opened and Dr Kharim and one of the wardsmen rushed in.

"Mr Dermid! What are you doing?" he asked.

Malvolio released me and tried to explain but the doctor cut him off. "Miss Callista needs to rest, Mr Dermid. She cannot be moving around like this with broken ribs."

I wasn't about to tell him they were healed. That wouldn't help me to get rid of Malvolio.

Malvolio looked shocked at the news — as if I hadn't already told him about it.

"Oh," he said innocently. "I didn't realise..."

I'd had enough of the charade. "Get him out of here!" I shrieked. "He was the one that *gave* me the broken ribs!"

CHAPTER 6

I Never Want to See You Again!

Malvolio tried to say it was an accident, that I'd had a fall, but I told them he'd kicked me while I was lying on the floor. He turned to me briefly with a look of such animosity and anger, a chill ran down my spine. The others hadn't caught it — it was only meant for me. I didn't want to even *think* what it meant, or what he would do the next time he saw me.

The wardsman asked him to leave, very politely, and eventually, he headed towards the door.

"I don't care if you're involved in the Talent programme here," I called after him. "I'm *not* your girlfriend anymore. I want to only deal with the doctors from now on. I never want to *see* you again!"

I knew he was livid, but I was so glad to see the back of him. I sunk down onto the bed and let only a few tears escape. I wouldn't cry over him.

I totally ignored the people in the room. It was way too late to be fussing over me and asking if I was okay.

Once I'd been left alone at last, I contacted Daniel.

I needed to talk to him.

After I told him what had happened, I sensed his anger.

"They should of done more to help you," he said. I tried not to let the tears escape. *"Just hang in there. We only have to wait a little bit longer till we can be free of Malvolio and Katoa and all the crap that goes with it. Then we'll be free to do whatever we want."*

That helped to calm me. I was looking forward to going home to see Mum and my not-so-little brother, Adamo, but mostly, I wanted — needed — to see Daniel again. It was great that we could still talk to each other, but besides the exhaustion that came with it, it wasn't the same as talking face-to-face. I wanted to be able to see him and to just fall into his arms.

Nearly losing him had shown me how much he meant to me. Thinking he was dead had done something to my heart. Like someone had wrenched it from my chest and put it back, but it wasn't quite the same anymore. Now I wanted to savour every moment with him and being kept apart was doing my head in.

My mind still wrestled with thinking I hardly knew him, then remembering I'd known him for months. It was going to take a long time to get my head around that.

I suppressed a yawn. *"I think I'd like to see your family first,"* I said. *"Taon is only a little closer than Azaeli, so it's on the way. Kind of."* I giggled.

Only a few million kilometres closer.

I tried to suppress another yawn, but failed. I had no idea what time it was. They'd moved me into a room that had a kitchenette and a small adjoining bathroom which meant I didn't have to leave the room for any reason and it was driving me crazy with nothing to do except answer more stupid questions and let them do their tests. Daniel had been moved too, and of course, we were both locked in for "our own safety."

It didn't make sense. We were both healed. We didn't need medical care. We should have been allowed to leave, then come back to the Infirmary for tests and to answer questions for their investigation.

I was starting to feel uncomfortable about it. Something was very wrong here.

"Okay," Daniel said. *"We can manage that. I'll introduce you to my family and show you my hometown. We could go sight-seeing too if you'd like."*

I took a deep breath and smiled. *"I'd like that."*

That was what we both needed. To be able to get to know each other better without anyone listening in or interfering. Without having to worry about what Malvolio might do. No rules dictating what we could and couldn't say.

"Once we're out of here, we'll be free," he said. *"As I've said, they can't keep us here. I'm going to keep on telling them till they let us go."*

"Me, too. They'll have to listen if we threaten to go to the Board of Employment. We can kick up a fuss with them. Katoa won't like that."

"Yeah. You know they still won't let me see the other Diggers that survived. It's ridiculous. I'd only have to walk down a hallway or two to visit them."

I sighed. *"They're so heartless. Those guys are your mates. Surely they could let you spend just a little bit of time with them. Cheer them up a bit."*

"Jacobi might be okay. They said he's got some broken bones and internal injuries. But Kassadan, I'm not sure. They said head injuries on top of broken bones and internal injuries. He might not pull through. They said family only, but he doesn't have family here. He's from Earth. It's so frustrating."

I was vaguely aware of the door swishing open in my room. Didn't anyone ever knock around here?

"Miss Callista?"

I groaned inwardly. It was my favourite doctor, Dr Rowen. *"I gotta go. Dr Rowen just burst in here."*

"Okay. Talk later."

I opened my eyes reluctantly. "Do you have to barge in here like that?"

"I didn't barge in."

"You waltzed in here without knocking. I'd say that's barging in."

She frowned. "What are you doing in bed at this hour?"

Geez. "I have no idea what time of day or night it is."

"We'll have to get you a clock."

"Plus, I was talking to Daniel."

"You should limit your communications with Mr Javolo until you've had some training."

As if I'm going to do that. "When can I go home so I can start my training?"

"That's what I'm here to speak to you about."

Good.

"We can start your training immediately while you're here at Perseus Station."

"What? You mean I'll get some pointers here before I go home?"

She tapped a finger on her leg. "No. You will receive all of your training through us."

"No! You can't do that! I'm only an employee — an ex-employee now. You have no right to keep me here."

I tried to sit up, but was hit by a wave of dizziness and had to lie back down.

She crossed her arms. "You have shown that you have a high T-Rating and you've been deemed too dangerous to be let go into the public space."

CHAPTER 7

Xander

"What? Are you serious?"

She crossed her arms. "Yes. Quite serious. You could harm yourself or others while wielding such power. By law, we have to keep you here and train you to control your Talent."

I resisted the urge to sit up. "You can't do this!"

"We can and we will."

"What about Daniel?"

"He is to be retained for training as well. His Rating is also quite high and is showing signs of being telekinetic. You will both be trained for your own good and the good of the community at large."

"No..."

My head was still spinning, and I didn't think it was only from trying to sit up. Surely there was a law against what they were doing. There had to be a way for us to get out of here and receive training back on our home planets.

"I want to call my mother."

She raised a manicured eyebrow. "Excuse me?"

"I want to speak to my mother and tell her what's going on."

The eyebrow came back down. "You're an adult. You do not need parental permission."

I rolled my eyes. "I know that. She needs to know what's happening. You can't deny me a Vid call."

She sniffed. "I'll see what I can do."

"No. Don't give me that Tauren shit. You'll arrange it. You can't stop me from talking to my own mother."

"Don't give me any lip, or I will *not* arrange anything for you."

I pursed my lips together. I didn't want to push it too far and miss out on talking to Mum.

I sighed. "So, what happens now?"

"Now, you will be introduced to your trainer and will learn control. That is of the utmost importance. We can't have you harming anyone."

"How can I harm someone? All I can do is speak telepathically to one person."

"Studies have shown that a person with a high T-Rating like yours has an eighty-five percent chance of developing multiple Talents once the first ability manifests. We need to be ready in case you show signs of telekinesis or other Recognised Talents."

I opened my mouth to tell her I hadn't shown any signs of telekinesis, but an image of my hairbrush on the floor and the Pegasus ornament that moved by itself flashed into my mind and I knew she was right. I had already manifested more than one Recognised Talent.

I decided not to tell her. Not yet, anyway.

There was a pause, and I let it all sink in. I'd have to stay on the station indefinitely. The thought made me nauseous.

"So when do I get out of here and go to wherever the training is? Because sitting in here doing nothing is driving me crazy. You've gotta let me out of this room."

"There's no need to move you from this room now."

"Why not? Do you conduct training in the Infirmary?"

"You're no longer in the Infirmary. You've already been moved to Katoa Labs."

"You moved me without telling me what's going on? Why would you do that?"

"This room is more suitable with the adjoining bathroom."

I squeezed my eyes shut. "So I'm stuck here in this room? I can't do that. I'll go mad."

"You will have designated rooms for training."

It was a relief to hear that I'd be getting away from these four walls, but I was anxious about what 'training' would actually entail.

"What am I expected to do for training?"

She sniffed. "That will be up to your trainer."

I wanted to sit up so I didn't have to look up at her, but I didn't want to faint. "That answer doesn't help me at all."

"That's all the answer I can give. I'm not the expert in Talent training. That is Xander's decision to make."

"Xander?"

She blinked. "Yes. Xander Zaleski. He will be your trainer."

His name sounded like an actor from a romantic HoloMovie and I tried not to giggle. "So when do I meet him and when do I start training?"

"Tomorrow morning at oh seven hundred. Someone will be here to collect you."

"Oh seven hundred? Geez. I didn't even have to start that early when I worked for you people."

"You will be required to be ready to go at the time specified and you will be giving your best during your training. We will not tolerate slackers. You will be trained as soon as possible to avoid any incidents with misuse of your Talent. Is that understood?"

"But—"

"Is that understood?"

"Yes."

Tomorrow was going to be a long day.

The next morning, I was ready at oh seven hundred. I was sure they'd only given me a clock so I could be ready on time.

My dreams were full of scenarios where I was either punched by Malvolio or hit by falling rocks in an underground tunnel, so I'd had a crappy night's sleep.

While I was getting ready, it occurred to me that they probably had cameras in my room. I retreated to the bathroom and tried to dress in a way that showed little of me to any camera that might be in there.

Someone actually knocked at the door once I was ready and I jumped. It swished open and I looked up at the broad-shouldered man standing in the corridor. He had an olive complexion, jet-black hair, and brown eyes that were so dark, they looked black.

Those eyes bored into mine. "Good morning, Miss Callista. I'm Xander Zaleski and I will be your trainer."

He looked about my age, which surprised me. I was expecting someone a lot older.

I'd had enough of people calling me Miss Callista. "Uh, hi. Please call me Lennina."

"Okay, Lennina. You ready to go?"

"Yes."

He turned on his heel and marched away. I assumed I was supposed to follow, so I walked quickly and tried to keep up with his long strides.

"Where are we going?"

"Somewhere we can train."

That's not very helpful.

I ran a hand through my hair, which I hadn't bothered tying back in a ponytail or bun now that I wasn't working. "What do I have to do?"

"You'll find out when we get there."

I sighed and gave up on asking any more questions.

He led me down a number of hallways and stopped at Room 623. I wondered how anyone could find their way around this place as all the doors and hallways looked the same.

Placing his thumb on the scanner, he turned and gestured for me to go in ahead of him as the door slid open.

I wasn't sure what to expect, but found myself in a small room with a table and two comfy chairs placed on either side of it.

"Please have a seat," he said.

Maybe I was expected to answer a whole bunch of questions. "What are we here for?"

"Training."

I raised my eyebrows at him. How were we supposed to train in this setting? What was 'training' anyway? I had a million questions.

He gestured to one of the chairs, so I reluctantly sat down. "We don't need much space or any specialised equipment to train." He sat in the other chair. "First, let's see what you can do."

"Um, I'm not sure how I can show you."

"What do you mean?"

I squirmed a little. "Well, so far, I've only been able to speak telepathically with one person."

He leaned back. "Yes. And?"

"Well, how do I show you that?"

He leaned forward. "You initiate a conversation with him or her right now."

My heartbeat picked up. "But how will you see that?"

He leaned forward some more. "I'll know."

"What?"

"I will monitor you."

I fidgeted nervously. "What does that mean?"

"I'll listen in."

My chest tightened. "No!"

"What's the big deal?" He smirked. "Do you have something to hide?"

"No. It's— I don't want you to listen in. That would be creepy." There's no way I wanted him listening to a private conversation between Daniel and I. "How can you do that, anyway?"

"I can connect with your mind first using a Mind-link, and then you'll contact the other person. Who is the other person?"

"Daniel Javolo. He's my Digger."

He raised an eyebrow as he leaned back again. "Your Digger?"

"Yes. I'm a Nav Operator... *Was* a Nav Operator. I quit."

He huffed. "That's not what it says in your file."

"What do you mean? I *am* a Nav. I've been a Nav for almost a whole rotation."

"No. Of course it says you're a Nav. It doesn't say you quit."

I rubbed my upper arm. "Well I did. The day of the collapse, I told Mr Sonrisa before my shift. Maybe it's because I hadn't given it to them in writing yet." I frowned. "So they're treating me like I still work for The Company?"

"Yeah. Seems so."

My fists clenched. I wanted nothing more than to get out of here.

Well, there was one thing: to see Daniel.

"I'll have to fix that. I did quit. I need a Palm-pad so I can make it official."

"Well, I don't know anything about it. I was just told to train you. There's nothing you can do to get out of that part. You can't be let go until you've learnt control."

"Yeah, I know. They told me."

He leaned forward again. "So, let's get started."

I cringed. "Now?"

"Yep." He let the 'p' pop.

My heart sped up again. "I can't just do it on command."

"You'll learn."

I ran a hand through my hair. "How does this work, then?"

He crossed his arms and leaned back. "I will initiate a Mind-link with you, then you'll contact your Digger."

I cringed. "But I don't know how to do a Mind-link."

"You don't need to do anything. Just relax your mind and I will take care of the rest."

I didn't like the sound of that. It was a scary prospect. What did a Mind-link entail? How much would he see inside my mind?

He smiled. "Let's go. Just relax."

I couldn't muster up a smile. I was terrified.

"Relax, Lennina. Let me into your mind."

I tried to relax, but it was hard.

"Close your eyes. Breathe slowly."

I did as he said, and I sensed something at the edge of my mind. Xander was trying to initiate the Mind-link, but I couldn't bring myself to let him past my defences. Up until that point, I didn't even know I had 'defences' in my mind.

"Let me in, Lennina. Don't fight me."

My shoulders tensed even more. "I... I can't."

"You can. Just do it."

"But... I don't know you."

I heard him shift in his seat. "What's that got to do with it?"

"It seems like such an intimate thing to do, and I only just met you. It's... wrong."

"Stop being so melodramatic. People do this all the time. It's just another way of communicating. It's no big deal."

I clenched my fists. "Well, it is to me!"

"Get off your high horse and just let me do this."

My eyes shot open and I stood up. "No!"

I was light-headed and grabbed the back of the chair for support.

He stood too. "Stop being so stubborn! It's not a big thing. You're not the one initiating it. It's easy. You just sit there and relax. Why can't you do that?"

I looked at his flushed face. "I told you. It feels wrong." I sunk back down in the chair.

"And I told you you're being melodramatic."

He pushed hard against my mind and I pushed back with as much force as I could.

His eyes widened and he lowered himself to his seat again. "How did you do that?"

CHAPTER 8
It Feels Like You're Looking Through Me into My Soul

"Do what? Push you away? Easy. Don't try to force your way in, Xander. That's wrong on so many levels."

His mouth was hanging open. "But, you shouldn't be able to do that."

"Well, I just did."

He rubbed his forehead with his hand. "Look, I'm supposed to train you, remember? You need to cooperate so we can get your training underway."

"I don't care. Can't you do it another way? Dr Kharim used an EEG. Can't we do that?"

"No. I have to observe what's actually going on. The EEG can't do that. It only monitors that there is activity in the brain."

"But—"

"No. I have to do this. You aren't getting out of here unless you let me in."

I glared at him for a long while, then sighed. I'd have to do this so I could get out of this place and see Daniel.

It wasn't fair.

I closed my eyes and tried to relax again. I felt him there, trying to find a way in, but the wall I'd built inside my mind held fast.

"Lennina," he warned.

"I know. I'm trying."

I concentrated on a section of the wall and willed it to fall away. Xander didn't waste any time and it was almost painful to let him in. My anxiety spiked. I felt vulnerable. Violated. How could he think this was just a normal, everyday thing? How could people do this and treat it so casually?

He started poking around and I tensed up. *"What are you doing? I thought you were just here to observe."*

"I am."

"It feels like you're looking through me into my soul."

"Maybe I am."

"Well, stop it."

"Relax, Honey. I'm not doing anything I'm not supposed to."

It didn't feel that way to me. *"So, now what?"*

"I've already told you. Strike up a conversation with whoever it is you can contact, and I'll observe."

"His name is Daniel."

"Okay, but I don't really need to know that."

I sighed. This guy didn't care about me or Daniel. He was just doing his job.

I tried to relax and concentrate. I hoped Daniel was awake. I'd already been through that circus with the doctors.

I reached out with my mind, hoping I could reconnect on-demand.

I went through some relaxation techniques and a few attempts to connect, then I finally found him. I quickly told him Xander was connected to my mind with a Mind-link and that he could hear our conversation. I needed to let him know before he said anything that could get us into trouble with The Company.

Well, *more* trouble.

Daniel wasn't happy about the situation. *"Is this really necessary?"*

Xander answered Daniel directly. *"Yes. I need to be able to observe what Lennina can do in order to have a starting point for her training."*

"Okay, but it seems a little... invasive."

"It is," I said. *"It feels... awful."*

Xander sounded frustrated. *"Stop being so melodramatic, Lennina. It's no biggie. I told you that."*

"And I told you that it is *a big deal to me. So leave me alone."*

He sighed. *"Geez. Don't get your shipsuit in a twist. I'm only doing my job."*

There was a pause and I tried to calm down, without much success.

I took a deep breath. *"So, now what?"*

"So, you guys do your thing. Talk or whatever. And I'll just sit here and watch."

His tone made it sound like he'd be watching us in the bedroom together or something. I shivered.

"I don't know what to talk about."

He shifted in his seat again. *"Talk about anything."*

"But it's weird with you listening."

"Just do it, okay. Then we can move on to something else."

I sighed. *"Okay. How have you been, Daniel?"*

"Good. Bored. There's nothing to do here and they won't even give me a Vid or a Palm-pad to pass the time."

I already knew this stuff, so I gathered he was saying it for Xander's benefit. Maybe something would be done about it, but I seriously doubted it.

"Yeah. Same here." What else was I supposed to say? Nothing had really happened since the last time we'd talked, so there was nothing to tell him. *"When are you starting your training?"*

"I've been told that someone will be here after lunch."

"Oh, okay."

Another pause.

"Daniel, your trainer is my partner, Sarinda," Xander said. *"She has a T3 Rating and is good at what she does."*

Xander hadn't told me his Rating, so I was curious. *"What's your Rating? Or is it rude to ask? I don't know how all this works."*

If he was offended, he didn't show it. *"I'm a T1. I was top of my class when I went through my Talent training."*

It sounded more like he was bragging than simply informing us. Something about his nature reminded me of Malvolio and that made me nervous.

"So, can we stop now?" I asked. I wanted him out of my head.

"I suppose so."

He sounded so casual about it all. It creeped me out having him in my mind. I wanted so badly to push him out of my head, but I knew it wouldn't do me any good. And I knew this was just the first time of many.

"So, I'll talk to you later, Daniel."

"Yeah, see ya, Cal."

My heart gave a little flutter at the sound of my nickname and I tried to keep my emotions under control. Daniel was the only person in the universe who'd ever called me Cal.

Once I felt that Daniel was gone, I turned my attention to Xander. *"Now, can you get out of my head?"*

"He calls you Cal?"

"Yes. Short for Callista. I want you out of my head."

"He shortened your surname? That's special."

"Shut up."

"Ooh. I've hit a nerve."

CHAPTER 9
You Will Practice on Me

And with that, he withdrew and it was a huge relief. I opened my eyes to find Xander staring at me with the hint of a smirk on his lips. I didn't find the situation funny at all.

He leaned back in his chair again. "You sure have your panties in a twist over this, don'tcha?"

"Which thing are you referring to?"

"Me being in your head."

"I don't care what you think, it's wrong."

The smirk grew. "You'll get used to it."

I didn't want to get used to it. "So, did you get what you needed to assess me?"

"Yes."

"And?"

"And," he paused and I was sure he did it to annoy me. "How do you feel?"

"What?"

"Do you ever feel exhausted after you've spoken to Daniel?"

"Every time I'm the one who starts the conversation. Why? What's wrong with me?"

"Probably nothing."

I resisted the urge to grab the edge of the table. "*Probably* nothing?"

"Well, I think you're initiating a Mind-link instead of just talking to him normally."

I frowned. "Normally? There's nothing normal about a telepathic conversation."

"Be careful what you say. Some people would take offence at that."

"Oh." I supposed they would. "Sorry. I've never been around people with Talent before and I don't know much about any of it."

"We'll have to educate you."

"Yeah." There was an awkward pause. "So. What do I have to do to fix it?"

"Huh?"

"How do I stop doing a Mink-link thing?"

"Oh, I'll teach you. You don't have to try so hard."

A wave of exhaustion swept over me and I wanted to lie down. "When can you teach me? I'd like to be able to do it without feeling like this..."

"I'd say now, but I think you need to rest first."

I had a feeling my training was going to last a lot longer than I'd first thought.

It was a huge relief to know I could talk to Daniel without using all my energy. They might have been able to keep us apart physically, but they couldn't stop us from using our Talent to talk to each other.

Once I'd recovered from using the Mind-link — which was after lunch — Xander took me back to that bland little room.

He went through some of the rules of the Talents' Code of Conduct regarding Talents with telepathic abilities. Apparently, there was a rule book stating how they — I mean we — should behave.

Normal people worried about a Telepath reading their minds without their knowledge or permission, which I could totally understand.

Telepaths were not permitted to read minds without permission, with a few exceptions — one of them being law enforcement. A Telepath was handy when it came to solving crimes as they could read a suspect's thoughts during an interrogation to see if they matched what the person was saying.

There were other rules too. Now that my Talent had manifested, I had to adhere to these rules.

I was given a copy of the Talents' Code of Conduct and was expected to read it. It was on a small device that was little more than a flexible screen and it contained nothing else. So no Palm-pad. Nothing I could use to amuse myself when I was stuck in that room alone.

I was getting antsy. This was interesting and important, but I needed to know how to talk to Daniel without fainting.

Xander crossed his arms over his broad chest. "Firstly, you need to learn how to shield your mind so others can't read your thoughts."

"How can I do that?"

"I'm supposed to teach you, but you've already shown you can keep people out. You have a natural talent for it."

I tensed up at the reminder. Having him in my mind was a horrible experience but I was glad I could keep him out even when he pushed hard.

"I'm not sure how I did it."

"I guess it doesn't matter how. You didn't seem to have a problem doing it."

No. When it came down to it, I was able to defend myself.

He finally went on to explain the way you would normally start a telepathic conversation and it wasn't as hard as I thought it would be. "You concentrate on their mind and you call them, but if you feel that thing where you're travelling through darkness, you know you've gone too far and you need to back off."

It made sense.

"It helps if the person is right in front of you so you can see their face."

My heart started pounding. "Are we going to bring Daniel in here so I can practice?" The thought of seeing him made me giddy.

"No. You will practice on me."

I tried to hide my disappointment. "But I've only ever spoken to Daniel."

"You've spoken to me."

"Yes, but I didn't initiate that conversation."

"It doesn't matter. It will still work."

I sighed. "Okay."

I'd have to be patient. I would see Daniel when my training was over. I was hoping for it to be sooner than that, but I doubted it.

Xander gave me some more tips, then leaned forward. "Now, concentrate on my face and try to speak to me." He pointed at his head.

I looked into his eyes and tried to ignore the urge to run out of the room. I had to focus. I wanted to be able to do this with Daniel, so I pushed myself.

After a few failed attempts, I was able to start a conversation with him.

"Am I doing it? I mean, without a Mind-link?"

"Yes."

I sighed. Then smiled. Now all I had to do was perfect this and I'd be outta here — and I'd be able to contact Daniel as easily as calling him on a Vid.

We practiced for a while and it was hard to find something to talk about. I wished it was Daniel I was talking to.

I was able to hold a conversation with my eyes open, while I moved around the room. It didn't use up half as much energy as a Mind-link.

Xander also said that once I got used to using my Talent, a Mind-link shouldn't use up so much energy and I would be able to do it without passing out. Apparently, when you get used to using a part of your mind you hadn't used before, it's a lot easier and less draining.

I smiled. That would be good. I was sick of passing out. I'd never had any problems with fainting before and had been pretty healthy for most of my life.

———— ★·☆·★ ————

Once we were finished, I was tired — which was apparently normal — but at least I didn't have to lie down to avoid fainting.

I smiled to myself. Today's lesson was a huge success.

I wondered what else I had to learn; I had the control bit sorted. I would probably be able to go home in a day or two.

Xander escorted me back to my cell — I mean, room — and he strolled back down the hallway like he owned the place as the door slid shut.

The first thing I wanted to do was contact Daniel. I concentrated until I was sure I wouldn't be creating a Mind-link.

"Daniel? Are you there?"

"Hey, you." There was a smile in his voice. *"Just eating dinner. How'd you go with What's-his-face?"*

"Xander," I supplied automatically. *"It went okay."*

I told him about the reason for my blackouts and that it looked like I wouldn't have the problem anymore.

"That's great. I was worried about you, especially when I didn't pass out, and neither did you when I initiated our conversations."

"I was starting to think there might be something seriously wrong with me. I'm glad that's not the case. It looks like I was going overboard and doing way more than I should have."

"Yeah. Sounds just like you."

I smiled. *"So, how did your training go?"*

"Oh, Sarinda went through some basics and we had a telepathic conversation or two, but it didn't really make me too tired. I practiced initiating a conversation and ending one. I think I did alright."

"That's good." That meant he'd be leaving soon too. *"I wonder what we're supposed to learn next. I mean, if we can start, hold, and end a conversation, what more do we really need to learn?"*

"I'm not sure. The rule book? But they don't really need to 'train' us for that. We can just read through it."

I wasn't sure what else we'd need after that. I wished I'd paid more attention to what I'd been told about the Talented during my schooling.

I looked around the room and wondered for the millionth time if there were cameras in here. *"Hey, do you think they have cameras in our rooms?"*

CHAPTER 10
You're Important to Me. You're Special

"I wouldn't be surprised. Arseholes. We'll have to be careful."

"It's creepy thinking that they can possibly be watching us while we shower."

"Yeah. Let's hope there's no cameras in the shower cubicles."

I cringed.

We talked about home and made some loose plans for what we wanted to do once we were free, and when we said goodnight and ended our conversation, I was able to walk around my room without passing out.

I fell asleep that night with a smile on my face.

———— ⋆ ☆ ⋆ ————

I looked around me and all I could see was dirt and rocks and tree roots. Above me, the sky was dark. Daddy would never find me.

A spider lowered itself from one of the roots. I cringed and moved further away so it wouldn't land on my leg.

A beetle crawled over my foot and I screamed.

I woke with a start and tried to slow my breathing. My heart raced. Would I ever get over being trapped in that hole in the ground when I was a child?

I hadn't thought about it for years, but Daniel being trapped under the ground had brought it all back to the surface.

I took a deep breath and as soon as my heartbeat slowed down, the alarm went off and sent it skyrocketing again.

Oh, hell.

I'd forgotten I had to get up at a ridiculous hour and do more training with Xander. I slowly dragged myself out of bed and used the bathroom.

As I exited the bathroom, Malvolio walked into my room and I gasped. "What are you doing?"

He frowned. "Good morning to you too, Lennina."

I clenched my fists. "You can't just walk in here!"

He smirked. "I just did, so I guess I can."

My heart raced. "I need to have some privacy in this place. Everyone just walks in here whenever they feel like it."

He looked down his nose at me. "You are here for training. We need to be able to see you and test you and look after you."

"Yeah, but I need privacy. What if I was naked? People need to knock!"

"If you have any requests, you'll need to take them up with Dr Rowen."

"I'm taking it up with you right now. You need to knock and wait for me to ask you in. It's only common decency."

"Okay, Lennina, darling. I'll do it for you."

"Don't call me darling," I spat. "I'm *not* your darling. And you shouldn't be here anyway. I still have that RO against you."

The memory of the night he assaulted me played on a loop in my mind and my heart rate picked up.

He sighed. "I don't know what to do. How can I get you to see that we were good together?"

The dark look in his eyes before he hit me flashed before my vision. "We weren't."

"Look, I'm sorry if I made you feel bad or unsafe. That was not my intention. I'm still dealing with some issues. You know my history. You know how my ex-partner broke me. She cheated on me. I walked in on them and was traumatised and devastated. I have so much trouble with trust now. She ruined things for me. I'm trying my best to overcome this, but it takes time. Time and the right person who is understanding and forgiving."

My chest was tight. "I can't be that person anymore. I'm sorry."

"You're important to me. You're special. You're such a powerful Talent now and your career options have skyrocketed. You have the universe at your feet."

It was starting to make sense. Now that he'd discovered I was a powerful Talent and I wasn't just a lowly Nav Operator anymore.

"I don't care what you say. I'm not going to change my mind."

"But why not?"

"You assaulted me."

"I never want to hurt you."

I clenched my fists again. "But you did."

His eyebrows shot up. "I have anger issues. I know this. You know this. My father was a hard man. Very harsh. He treated everyone badly. He wasn't a good role model for me when I was a young man. No wonder I turned out the way I did. I can change. With you. Things are different with you. I'm different with you. You make me a better man. I can better myself. I can strive to be a better man."

I sighed. "But I can't be with you anymore. I can never trust you again."

"Trust me? But I've been nothing but good to you. You can trust me with your life. I made one stupid mistake and you're going to doom me forever." He stepped forward.

"That one 'stupid mistake' wasn't something small or trivial. I had three broken ribs."

Another step forward. "I know you're a loving and compassionate person, Lennina. I know you can find it in your heart to forgive me."

I resisted the urge to take a step back. "No. I can't."

"You just need to give me a chance."

I frowned. "No."

His eyes were pleading. "I can prove it to you. I will be the perfect gentleman. You'll see."

"But I've told you; I don't want you to be my boyfriend anymore."

A frown creased his brow. Was he finally getting it?

"It's him, isn't it?"

CHAPTER 11

Don't Change, Cal. Not for Him. Not for Anyone

"Daniel? Yes. It is."

He narrowed his eyes. "I knew it. It's been him all along."

I started to pace the room. "No. Last time I hadn't even met him. We were just friends working together."

"He's so beneath you, darling. You know this."

"Don't call me darling. And he is *not* beneath me. I'm not concerned with status like you are. I don't care what job he has or where he came from or how many credits are in his account. It has nothing to do with any of that stuff. That's what you don't understand. You never understood. You never really knew me at all, did you?"

He threw his hands up. "Of course I did! I know you better than he does. Better than anyone in the universe."

I stopped pacing. "Uh, no. You don't. You didn't bother to get to know who I really am. You only knew the person you wanted me to be."

"Forget him."

"Why are you suddenly so interested in having me back? It's because I'm a Talent, isn't it?"

He'd already said as much.

His eyebrows shot up again. "No. Of course not. Don't be ridiculous. We have chemistry, you and I. We were meant for each other."

"No. We're not. Just go. Leave me alone."

The frown was back. "Don't tell me what to do."

"You're wasting your time, Malvolio. I will *never* go back to you."

"You will regret that decision."

And with that, he spun on his heel and walked out of the room.

He was a whirlwind. He left carnage behind every time I spoke to him.

I had to talk to Daniel again after that. I didn't care that Xander was on his way.

It was easier that time to reach his mind and I told him what had happened.

"He's an arsehole," Daniel said, and I sensed his anger. *"Somebody needs to stop him. He can't be allowed to walk into your room like that. You have an RO out against him, for fuck's sake."*

"Everyone seems to just waltz in here whenever they bloody feel like it. Even Rowen."

I realised I was digging my fingernails into my palms, so I took some deep breaths to try to calm down.

"They do it to me too," he said. *"But if Malvolio tries it, I'm gonna deck him."*

"He deserves it. He's just... I don't know. I should've seen it sooner. There were all these signs, and I didn't see them."

"Don't beat yourself up about it now. He's a master manipulator. And that part of your life is in the past. You've told him how you feel."

"I know. I just wish I could get away from him. I'm stuck in here with no way to escape from his crap." I sighed. *"I wish I'd never met him. And what I said to him is true. He didn't know me. He was never really interested in anything I did, you know? Not interested in my family or my love of music. When I talked about you or stuff about work, he would get so agitated. I couldn't understand it. I started to think that maybe he was jealous of you, but being jealous of someone I'd never meet was ridiculous. But then he kept getting worse. Sometimes I would just stop myself from telling him about my day so I could avoid the drama."*

I sniffed. My cheeks were wet.

I was kind of blabbering on, but I couldn't help it. *"And I never felt comfortable when we went out with friends — probably because they were his friends. I always felt out of place. I tried to improve the way I talked and bought some nicer clothes — even bought some dresses — but it didn't change anything."*

"Don't change, Cal. Not for him. Not for anyone."

"But—"

"I mean it. You're perfect just the way you are." There was a smile in

his voice. *"Don't change any of the things I love about you."*

A smile spread across my face.

The smile soon faded. Talking about Malvolio was making me queasy so I decided to change the subject. *"We need to tell the authorities about the Ghosts."*

"Yes."

"They're called Ampari."

"Ampari. That's good to know."

I frowned. *"We need to work out who to tell first. It needs to be someone who's not working for Katoa or for Malvolio or someone that doesn't know him. They all seem to adore him or are scared of him. Or both."*

"You think so?"

CHAPTER 12
I Choose to Be Here

"Yes. Believe me. I've seen it. Just look at how they wouldn't help me in the Infirmary or in here."

"Yeah. You're right. And I'd like to punch him in the throat for that." There was a pause. *"We need to contact someone on Earth. Starfleet Federation about the Ampari and the Board of Employment about how we've been treated."*

I nodded, then realised he couldn't see me. *"Yes."*

"We will organise it soon. Right now, we need to rest. We'll work out what needs to be done and what we should be doing first..."

"Yeah."

"Tomorrow. We'll work stuff out tomorrow," he said.

We said our goodbyes and I felt a little better.

———— ★·☆·★ ————

Xander had been scowling at me all morning because I hadn't been ready when he'd turned up at the door. After what had happened with Malvolio, I was past caring about being on time for training.

We were sitting in the stupid training room again and my mind wandered. I wondered why I hadn't seen Allador. It hadn't been that long since he'd healed me, but I couldn't help wondering what was happening with him and his people.

I looked around at the white walls. I hated this room already.

I thought I'd try to spark up a conversation instead of sitting here in silence.

"So, what did you do before they locked you up in here?"

His eyes snapped to mine. "I'm not locked up. I choose to be here."

My eyes widened. "What? Why?"

He sat up straighter. "They're doing studies here that can't be done anywhere else in the universe. They're trying to find out where the Lightning comes from. No one else has reported the same phenomenon anywhere in the Known Universe. They think it has something to do with the close proximity to the Amakio."

That made sense. It could be the Amakio. I wondered if the Ampari had something to do with it too. They had telepathic and telekinetic abilities and were made of energy.

He leaned back in his seat. "So, to answer your question, I was a shuttle pilot. I probably flew Javolo down to the planet a bunch of times."

"How did you know you had Talent?"

"I started hearing people's thoughts all around me. I thought I was losing it, till I realised what was going on. And now I think it's awesome."

I tried to imagine being bombarded with everyone's thoughts at once. I was glad it didn't happen to me. "What about Sarinda? How did you two meet?"

"She was a tech working for Galaxy Mech. I'd see her in the docking bay all the time when she was working with the Diggers."

"That's cool. So how long have you been together?"

"About a year. We both developed Talent at about the same time, formed the Lightning Connection, then started showing signs of telekinesis not long after."

Now he had my attention. "How did you form the Connection?"

"It happened the first time we touched, really. I felt a jolt of electricity and a buzzing sensation."

I gasped. That was exactly how it happened with Daniel and I.

"The same happened to you, huh?"

"Yeah."

And not long after was when I started to move things by accident with my mind.

I thought it was time to tell someone about it. Rowen had said it could become dangerous if I didn't learn to control it.

I sighed. "I suppose I should tell you."

"Tell me what?"

"There've been instances where something has moved without me touching it."

He raised his eyebrows. "Why haven't you mentioned this before?"

"I don't know. I wasn't sure what it was at first. I thought maybe I'd imagined it."

He leaned forward. "We need to test you right away."

"How do we do that?"

"You need to try to move something."

"But I don't know how I did it."

"We'll start with something small. Size has no bearing on whether you can lift something or not, but it's all psychological. If your brain thinks the object is light and easy, it will be more willing to accept the fact that it can lift it."

That made sense.

I ran a hand through my hair. "But I don't know how—"

"I will teach you. That's what I'm here for."

He pulled a personal Com from his pocket and placed it on the table.

"That should do. Now, get comfy. Close your eyes. Imagine the Com in your mind. The shape. The weight. Get a really good image of it. Now imagine lifting it into the air."

I took a deep breath and did as he said. I imagined me pushing it upwards and holding it suspended in the air.

"Don't open your eyes. Start again. Imagine it again. As if you're picking it up with your hand. Lift your hand up and take the Com with it. Now hold it there."

I did it again. And thought maybe I'd done it.

I opened my eyes to find that it hadn't moved.

"Close your eyes and try again."

"But I can't do it. I don't know what I'm doing."

"Did you expect to get it on the first or second try? Keep going."

I took a deep breath. He was right. Closing my eyes again, I concentrated. I could do this. I'd made those things move before. I needed to be able to do it on purpose now.

"Again."

I kept trying and failing.

"Again."

"This is stupid," I said as I ran my fingers through my hair.

The Com slid across the table toward Xander and I gasped.

CHAPTER 13

I've Something to Tell You Both

"There. You *can* do it. Try again."

Okay. I can do it. I just did it.

I tried again, pushing just a little bit harder.

"Now open your eyes."

This time, the Com was floating about ten centimetres above the table's surface. I'd done it!

It fell back onto the table with a clatter as I lost concentration. "Oops! Sorry."

"We'll work on that. It's extremely important that you learn control and never drop what you're lifting."

That made perfect sense. My mind supplied a dozen images of things falling out of the air and crashing to the floor. I could do some real damage if I wasn't careful.

"Got it."

Later that day, Dr Rowen actually came through and let me call home.

Adamo answered; Mum wasn't home. I was so glad to see him and wanted to tell him everything, but Dr Rowen had told me I couldn't give anyone details regarding an ongoing investigation.

"So." How did I even explain? "There's been a couple of changes since I last spoke to you and Mum."

He frowned. "You're not going out with that jerk again, are you? 'Cause if you are, I'm gonna kick your arse!"

"No, nothing like that. Keep your hair on."

"What is it, then?"

"I'm going to come home early. It looks like I've developed some Talent and I need training."

"What? How? What kind of Talent?"

"Telepathy and telekinesis."

"Oh, wow! That's... that's off the planet, Nina! Wait till I tell Mum. How did it happen?"

"I don't know. It was pretty sudden. I've started training here because they say someone with no control over their Talent can be dangerous."

"Oh. I guess they could. Have you done anything 'dangerous?' Have you accidentally hurt someone?"

"No. I only learned how to lift something today."

A smile spread across his face. "That's so spaced. I wonder if I'll inherit something like that."

"I don't know. Maybe you will."

"So, when are you coming home?"

I rubbed my forehead. "I don't know. I wanna come home now, but my training looks like lasting a long time."

His eyebrows drew together. "But they can't keep you there. You can train here at home."

"That's what I told them, but they won't let me transfer. They reckon I'm gonna hurt someone."

He ran a hand through his spiky hair. "That's crud. I'm gonna tell Mum. We'll sort something out, okay?"

"Okay. If you can organise a transfer to our nearest TTF Centre, that would be so awesome."

Behind Adamo, the door slid open and Mum walked into the room. Adamo turned away from the Vid and told Mum what I'd told him, but instead of being happy for me, she burst into tears.

"Mum! What's wrong?" Adamo and I asked together.

It took a while to pull herself together. "I hoped this would never happen, but now that it has, I've something to tell you both."

I frowned. "What is it?"

"It's about your father—"

"I don't want to hear about him—"

"I need to tell you. About why he left."

"He's a deadbeat—"

"No. He's not. I guess I can tell you now. It doesn't matter anymore. He left to protect you and Adamo. In case you had the same marker that he'd found in his own DNA."

CHAPTER 14
You Could Have Told Us

"What?"

"He didn't just randomly leave us one day, and there wasn't another woman or anything like that. He loved us all very much, and that's why he left. He knew that if the authorities found out about the unusual DNA marker, they'd want to take him away for testing, just like they're doing to you now, and that they'd want to test you and Adamo to see if you had the same marker."

"But he didn't know for sure if we had the marker? He didn't test us?" She shook her head. "Why not?"

"Because then there'd be a record of the results."

That made sense. This new information rushed through my mind, rearranging all the memories relating to my father.

That's why he left so suddenly and why I couldn't remember any arguments between my parents before he left. That's why she let him go and didn't say anything as he walked out the door.

But I couldn't bring myself to forgive him for leaving. Years of hating him was hard to change. He ruined our family.

"Surely he didn't have to leave. Couldn't we have gone with him?"

"And lived in hiding? We would've had to leave everything and everybody we knew behind. We would've been travelling from place to place, not knowing where we'd be going next. It would've been a terrible life for you both. We didn't want that for you. Your father did the right thing."

My chest ached. "You could have told us."

Her eyes filled with fresh tears. "I couldn't risk anyone finding out."

"You still love him?"

She wiped a tear from her cheek. "Yes. I still love him."

Dr Rowen walked into the room and tapped her watch.

I turned back to the Vid. "Umm. I gotta go now, but I'll call you soon, okay?"

The look on the doctor's face told me I wasn't going to be calling home anytime soon.

Mum sniffed and cleared her throat. "Okay, Honey. I'll see what we can do at this end, alright?"

"Yes, okay. Thanks, Mum. Thanks, Shorty. Love ya. Bye."

"Love ya. See ya." They both said.

I hoped Dr Rowen hadn't heard our conversation, but there was nothing I could do about it if she did. It didn't matter anymore now that I'd developed Talent and they knew about the DNA marker.

I ended the call and glared at her. "I want a transfer to my local TTF."

"No."

"No? You can't refuse. My mother will apply for me and I'll be going home. I've learned enough self-control to make it back home without hurting anyone."

"You will not be going anywhere until Xander and myself approve."

I opened my mouth. Closed it. Clenched my fists. Took a deep breath, stood and strode out of the room. As I walked, I heard what sounded like the Vid screen hitting the floor.

That was really going to help support my argument of having self-control.

I tried to calm down after walking out on Dr Rowen, without any success.

I was done with it. The whole lot. I was only an employee. They couldn't keep me here like a prisoner.

Rowen was an idiot. Xander was arrogant. Malvolio was a jerk. And he was so volatile. He scared me.

I had to get out of here.

Since Xander hadn't followed me out of the room, I had a chance to do something about my situation as I walked down the hallway leading to the cafeteria. I turned away from the cafeteria and hoped I could find a way out before too many people noticed I wasn't where I was supposed to be.

As I walked, I thought about my conversation with Mum. I still couldn't believe she'd let Adamo and I think our father had deserted us for no reason. My heart rate picked up.

Why? Why did she do that? I loved him once. With all my heart. How could she let me grow to hate him?

I didn't want to hate him. I wanted things to go back to the way they were before he left.

I didn't understand. I wanted out. I needed to run.

After a few more corridors, I felt disheartened. Where was the way out? How big was this place?

I passed a woman in a blue uniform. What did the blue mean? What was her job here? Everyone seemed to have a specific colour for their role at Katoa Labs. She stared at me, but didn't say anything.

I kept walking and hoped she wouldn't tell security.

A couple of corridors later and a man wearing a blue uniform similar to the woman's saw me and called out.

I ignored him and turned a corner.

"Miss? Wait! You shouldn't be here. Are you lost?"

I hurried around another corner and almost ran into a nurse wheeling a cart filled with medical equipment.

"Sorry!"

I darted around her and kept going.

"Hey! You can't go that way!"

A quick glance behind me showed that she'd stayed with the cart, but the man was now running toward me, calling out as he went.

I broke into a run.

The man called security on his personal Com. My heart thundered in my chest, and not just because I hadn't had enough exercise lately.

As I approached a corner, two men came out in front of me and my first instinct was to push out with my arms. They flew backwards, landing on their backs and sliding across the floor.

I was shocked that I'd managed to do that. I just wanted them to keep away from me.

This telekinesis could come in handy.

I kept going. The man behind me had gained some ground while I'd stopped to deal with the other men.

"Stop!"

I pushed some energy behind me and heard him fall over as I kept running.

There was a doorway ahead. It looked like a possible way out. There were three men standing in front of it, but I was sure I could deal with them.

When I got within ten metres of them, a jolt of lightning that was much stronger than the jolt I'd felt whenever I touched Daniel slammed into my back. I lost control and hit the floor hard, legs and arms flailing around, thinking I must have been hit with a stunner.

CHAPTER 15

You're in Deep Shit Now, Darlin'

As the convulsions stopped, Xander's face came into view. "What are you trying to do, Lennina?"

"You can't keep me here. It's against Intergalactic Law."

Lightning circled his hands. He'd zapped me with Lightning. "This again. We've told you. We can keep you here until you're trained and are no longer a danger to yourself or anyone else."

"I've learnt control. I can continue training on Azaeli. You can't stop me from going home."

"We can and we will. Dr Rowen and I will decide when you can leave. And that little demonstration back there with the Vid just proves you're not ready."

He reached out and touched my cheek and a jolt that was about half the strength of the one I got from Daniel ran through me. I sucked in a breath and his eyebrows rose.

"The Lightning is strong in you. I can feel it. Stronger than when I touch any of the others." He pulled his hand away. "That's weird."

How many others were there?

I was dragged to my feet by two security guards, who pulled my arms behind me and slapped on some handcuffs.

Xander smirked. "You're in deep shit now, darlin'."

He turned on his heel and I was forced to follow with a guard holding each arm.

After too many turns to keep track of, we arrived at a door that looked like every other door in this place. Inside was basically an interrogation room. A table with two chairs.

Dr Rowen entered the room with a scowl on her face as Xander slipped out the door. She didn't ask me to sit, so I remained standing.

"We give you free accommodation and free training and this is how you repay us?"

I scowled back at her. "You can't keep us here. It's illegal."

"It is not illegal. We are required to teach you control."

"You have taught us control. You can't keep us here indefinitely. I need to call my mother. I need a lawyer."

"You need to be taught a lesson. And you haven't learnt control. You damaged a Vid screen on your way out."

"Who said that was an accident?"

It was, but I wasn't going to tell her that.

Her expression darkened. "Like I said, you need to be taught a lesson."

"You can't touch me."

"We can. We can do whatever is necessary to train you."

I lifted my chin defiantly. "I don't care what you do to me."

"As I said; we can do whatever is necessary."

I huffed. "You can't touch me."

"Oh, we're not going to touch you."

Pain exploded across my cheek. "What... ?"

It took a few seconds to realise what had happened; someone had hit Daniel.

She smirked. "Yes. That's right. We know you can feel his pain."

Tears stung my eyes. "Why are you hurting Daniel? I was the one that tried to escape. He had nothing to do with it. Leave him alone."

She leaned forward and looked into my eyes. "You said you don't care what we do to you, so I thought you'd probably care what we do to him."

"That's not fair."

She straightened. "Life's not fair."

Pain exploded across my other cheek, followed by what felt like a punch to the gut. My stomach muscles tensed as if I'd actually been hit and I gasped for breath. "You bitch! Stop it right now!"

"You need to learn. You can't escape and you can't go around hurting members of my staff."

I thought maybe if I agreed with her, they'd stop hurting Daniel. "Okay. I won't do it again."

"I don't believe you."

The pain started again and I was hit by a barrage from many directions and all I could think of was that they were doing this to Daniel. He'd be the one with the bruises and the bloodied lip. I squeezed my eyes shut and waited for it to stop.

When it finally ended, I was lying on the floor with my legs drawn up around me and my hands still cuffed behind my back. She sighed in disgust as she strode out of the room.

———— ★·☆·★ ————

The following day, Daniel and I were speaking telepathically and I was telling him what my mother told me when Rowen barged into my room and told me I had been assigned a guide to help me find my way around the facility.

I told Daniel what she'd said.

"What a load of Tauren crap," he spat.

A man with dark skin and black, curly hair stepped into the room from behind Dr Rowen and she gave me her fake smile. "Raynar will be your guide here at Katoa Labs as Xander has a busy tutoring schedule at the moment. Wherever you need to go, let Raynar know and he will take you there."

Yep. Definitely Tauren crap. "Don't you mean guard?"

The smile stayed in place. "No. He's your guide."

I rolled my eyes. "If you say so."

Rowen ignored me. "Raynar is a Telepath. We assign Talents to guide other Talents. It helps the new trainees relax more to have someone they can relate to."

"You mean, a Talent has a chance of stopping another Talent from trying to escape again."

She sniffed. "He will stop you. You can count on that."

"I got me a guard dog too," Daniel informed me.

"Mine's name is Raynar. What's yours?"

"Baudin. He's a Kinetic."

Raynar's dark eyes turned my way. *"Raynar is a Telepath. He looks like he's trying to see into my brain right now."*

CHAPTER 16

What if it Wasn't Even Real?

"Don't let him intimidate you."

I glared at him.

I sensed him trying to get into my head, but it was easy to keep him out. I didn't know what his T-Rating was, but if Xander was a T1, then I guessed that I could keep any other T1 out, as well as anyone with a lower Rating.

Raynar's face twisted. He wasn't happy that he couldn't read my mind. I smiled.

"He can't get past my defences," I told Daniel.

"That's good. He won't be able to see what we're planning."

Rowen said she would leave us to it and strode out the door. I wondered why Raynar didn't tell her he couldn't get into my head. Maybe he was embarrassed. He would have to have a high Rating for them to assign him as my guard. Was he worried he'd lose his job if he told them?

Probably. I had no idea how things worked in this place.

He looked at his wrist. "It is time for you to start your training. Let's go."

I folded my arms. "I do know the way, you know."

He turned on his heel and marched out the door. "Follow me."

This was going to be so much fun.

The next couple of days of training were not a pleasant experience. I was still seething from what they'd done to Daniel and was still feeling the bruises. From Daniel's description, I was pretty sure Xander had been the one delivering the blows, so he was the last person I wanted to be spending my days with.

We'd alternated between telepathy and telekinesis and I felt I had a pretty good grasp of it. I could initiate and hold a conversation without using a Mind-link and I could initiate a Mind-link on purpose. And when I did, I didn't feel half as exhausted as I had initially.

I felt more confident and could lift a variety of objects without dropping them. I should have been feeling proud of my achievements, but it was overshadowed by the fact that they were keeping us prisoners.

Sitting across from Xander in our boring little training room, I sighed. "When can I go home?"

Xander sighed too. "Not this again. When are you gonna shut up and listen? I'm trying to train you so you *can* go home."

"But I've learnt control. I don't accidentally lift stuff. I don't drop things. I don't accidentally do Mind-links anymore. I don't hear everyone's thoughts like you did at first. I'm not dangerous."

"That is for me and the doctors to determine."

"I'm sick of hearing that."

"Just shut up and move this block to the corner of the room."

I felt like hurling it at his head, but I moved it without any difficulty or dropping it and sighed again.

His frown deepened. "Stop with the sighing."

I sighed louder just to annoy him.

"You need to lose the attitude and take all of this seriously."

I rolled my eyes.

Xander looked me in the eye. "Listen. I'm serious. You need to lose that attitude or you'll never truly learn control."

That sounded like Tauren crap to me, but I didn't respond. I needed to let him think I would behave. I had to get out of here.

He leaned closer. "What everyone can't understand about you two is how you got your Lightning Connection."

I was thrown by the abrupt change of subject. "What do you mean?"

"How'd you get it without touching each other? Everyone else here got it through physical contact, but you were showing signs before he touched you in the Infirmary."

How did he know so much about what had happened?

"How many people have the Lightning thing?"

"Fourteen now that you and Digger Boy have arrived."

"Digger Boy? Really? That's all you could come up with?"

"Give me time. I'll think of something better."

I smirked. "You're not very good at this."

He huffed out a breath and looked at me. "So, you gonna tell me how you did it?"

I shrugged. "We met before the Infirmary," I told him. "We ran into each other at a restaurant on the station and didn't know we were work partners. You know the rules. I thought he worked for Galaxy Mech or something."

I hoped Daniel wouldn't get upset with me for telling Xander, but I figured they'd probably work it out sooner or later by watching camera feeds on the station or something.

I cringed thinking about when the two eggheads from Katoa would be coming back to interview me again.

"So, Danny Boy broke the rules and sneaked over to the other section?" Xander rubbed his chin. "I'm impressed."

I raised an eyebrow. "Danny Boy?"

"I'll get there."

I couldn't help smiling. "He just wanted to see what the rest of the station looked like before he went home."

"Sure he did. But look what happened. He didn't go under the radar. He went and sparked up a relationship with you. *Literally*." He laughed at his own joke.

"I'm not sure you could call it a relationship just yet."

He leaned back. "Oh, believe me, it is, whether you like it or not. The Lightning forms a Connection and you're stuck with the other person and there's kinda nothing you can do to stop it. Didn't they tell you any of this stuff?"

I frowned. "No. Rowen tells me nothing."

"Don't worry about it. From what I've seen, Danny Boy isn't bad lookin'. You'll be okay with him."

"What do you mean by stuck with him?"

"I mean the Connection is hard to break; some people weren't a couple before the Lightning, but now they are."

I frowned again. What if I'd felt such a strong connection to Daniel because of the Lightning? What if it wasn't even real? What was I supposed to do with that?

Chapter 17

We Need a Plan

Xander let me stew on that for a while, then sat up straighter. "Now I'm gonna teach you some defence stuff."

That got my attention. "What?"

"You can use your Talent to protect yourself. You can push people away from you — as you've already discovered — or use objects to attack them. I can show you how if you'll stop grumbling long enough to learn it."

I sat forward. "Teach me."

He explained that the principles were still the same as what I'd already learned; I just had to adapt them to the situation at hand. I could throw the block I'd just placed in the corner at him — which was kinda hilarious because I'd thought about doing it — push him to the floor, or hurl sharp objects at an enemy.

I pictured me hurling the block at his head.

But on the serious side; this could be useful.

He gave me some pointers and we got started.

———— ★·☆·★ ————

After I'd finished my training session and had some dinner, I contacted Daniel while Raynar was tagging along next to me. It was frustrating not being allowed to see Daniel, but fantastic to talk to him whenever I wanted.

I explained how Xander was teaching me defensive stuff. *"But I want him to teach me how to use the Lightning to attack, like he did to me."*

"Yeah. That's freaky, but it could be very useful if we wanna get out

of here."

"Maybe that's why he's not showing me how to do it."

"We might have to work out how to do it on our own. Or convince them to tell us. I'll work on Sarinda while you work on Xander."

"Yeah, okay. Because I wanna get out of here as soon as possible. I don't want to wait till they say we're fully trained. The way things are going, we'll never get out of here."

"We'll get out of here soon."

I had serious doubts about that.

We arrived at my room and Raynar planted himself outside as the door slid shut. I was glad he didn't come in.

"So, Xander said something about the Lightning Connection. First he wanted to know how we formed a Connection without touching, so I told him we'd met before we touched in the Infirmary. I don't want them thinking we're some kind of miracle case or we'd never get out of here. I hope you don't mind. They probably would have found out sooner or later anyway."

"I guess they would have. I don't want to stay here any longer than we have to. Don't worry about it. What else did he say?"

"He said every couple that forms the Connection are kinda stuck with each other. Even if they weren't a couple before they touched, they are now."

"Okay. That makes sense I guess."

I ran a hand through my hair. *"So, what if it's not real?"*

"What if what's not real?"

"What if this thing between us is just the Connection and not anything we feel for each other?"

"Hey, don't go there. Don't forget that we knew each other and fell for each other long before we touched."

"Oh, yeah." Relief flooded through me. I'd been more worried about it than I'd realised. *"Duh. Now I feel silly."*

"Don't feel that way. This is all new to both of us. We need to get our heads around it."

"You got that right." I clenched my fists. *"And we need to get out of here."*

"Yes. But we need a plan. You can't go charging toward the exit without some kind of plan in place."

"I know. It was stupid." I hung my head. *"I'm really sorry."*

"Hey, you didn't know they were gonna beat me up for it."

"I still feel really bad."

"I'm almost healed. I've been through a lot worse, remember? I'll be fine."

I remembered. I shivered as a chill ran up my spine. The utter devastation I'd felt as his Mech-suit ran out of air when he was trapped underground made my heart hurt. It washed over me. I never wanted to feel that way again. I couldn't handle it.

I sunk down onto my bed. I suddenly needed to sit down. *"I gotta go. I'll talk to you tomorrow."*

"Are you okay? It's only early."

"Yeah, I just need some sleep. I'm tired."

"Okay. Talk tomorrow. We'll try to form some sort of plan, okay? We've learnt control. We can talk like this whenever we want. But we need to learn to block each other's pain. We need an escape plan. And we still need to tell people about the Ampari and the air situation."

"Okay. Yes. You're right. Goodnight."

"Goodnight."

Guilt washed through me. Why did I do that? I wasn't too tired to talk. I shook my head and wandered into the bathroom to wash my face and get ready for bed.

I looked across to the locked door on the opposite side of the bathroom. Why was it there? It made no sense.

It irked me that there was a door there that they could unlock at any time and walk in on me in the shower or something. I wished I could lock it — and my other door — from the inside to keep them all out.

I glared at the door. What possible reason could there be for having a door there? Was there another room on the other side? Did they have it set up so that if someone was in there they'd have to share this bathroom with me? If so, I hoped no one moved in there. The last thing I needed was to have to share a bathroom with a total stranger.

I cringed as I imagined having to share a bathroom with Xander.

—— ★·☆·★ ——

I sat myself down in the comfy chair in the counsellor's office. He introduced himself as Dr Lysander.

This'll be good.

There'd been no warning, just a message to go to see the counsellor at 0900 this morning.

"So, Miss Callista, how are you feeling today?"

That was so cliché. I resisted the urge to roll my eyes. How was I going to take this seriously? "Lennina. Please. And I'm fine, considering the circumstances."

"Okay, Lennina. What circumstances would that be?"

My eyes wandered to the walls where there were numerous certificates and awards prominently displayed. "Daniel and I are being held here against our will and should be allowed to go home to complete our training."

He steepled his hands and looked at me. "What makes you think that you are ready to go home?"

"We were told that we needed to learn control and we've done that. We're not a danger to anyone. We can finish our training back on our home planets."

"Dr Rowen and Xander Zaleski are working closely together to make sure you get the best training available. You need to respect that. They only have your best interests at heart."

Tauren crap. "Yeah. Sure they do."

"So. Can I ask you some questions?"

No. "Sure."

He led with the obvious. How I ended up getting the job with Katoa and what were my plans for the future and blah, blah, blah. I answered them all and tried not to squirm in my seat.

He moved on to my childhood and home life and of course, once I got to the bit about my father leaving, he was very interested.

"How do you feel about your father now?"

Seriously? Were all counsellors in the universe the same? "How would *you* feel?"

"That's not really relevant. I need to know how *you* feel."

After my conversation with Mum, those feelings were a jumbled mess.

"I hate him for leaving. He just walked out the door and we never heard from him again. Who does that?"

I bit my lip. I needed to shut up. I'd just given him a whole heap of ammunition.

CHAPTER 18

Lose the Attitude, Lennina

"So you haven't had any contact with him since you were eight?"

Oh, boy. "No. I just said that."

"Would you like to talk about the way you feel?"

"No."

"Would you like to talk about what you believe a parent should do to nurture their children?"

"No."

I shouldn't have told him anything.

"How are you feeling now that we've been delving into your past?"

"Like a million credits."

"Lennina. You are meant to take these sessions seriously."

"Sessions? With an 's'? How many sessions are we talking here, Doc? I have a busy schedule, you know. Gotta learn how to not kill people with my out-of-control Talent."

"It will be as many as it takes. Longer if you don't lose the bad attitude."

"That's funny. My supervisor back in Navigational Operations told me I have a bad attitude too."

The good doctor squeezed the bridge of his nose. I was starting to get to him.

Good.

"Lennina, we can work on that in these sessions if you'd like."

"What's there to work on? This is me. Take it or leave it."

He took a deep breath in through his large nose. "You need to improve that attitude if you want to work for Katoa."

"Well, that's the thing. I don't. I quit."

Lysander's eyebrows rose. "You resigned? I don't have anything about that in your file."

"No. Neither did Xander. I quit the day of the collapse. Only it was verbal. I didn't get a chance to do a written one."

"Okay. Well, I'll add a note in here about that."

"Yeah, you do that. No one else has. They all want to pretend that it didn't happen." I leaned forward in my seat and waved a finger at him. "And don't ask me how I feel about that, or I might just zap your arse."

His eyebrows rose again. "Is that a threat?"

"Yeah, but only a half-hearted one. It wouldn't be worth the trouble I'd be in." Guilt crashed over me when I thought of them hurting Daniel again.

Lysander sighed. "Why don't we leave it there for today and you can come and see me again when you can take this seriously?"

"What makes you think I'm gonna take this seriously next time? Or ever?"

He sighed again. "I will make another appointment for you. You can return to your normal training for the rest of the day. Take care and I will see you soon."

"I hope not."

"Lose the attitude, Lennina. It will not serve you well while you're in here."

"I don't care."

Five days later when I'd finished getting ready in the morning, the door swished open and Malvolio stood there with a sad look on his stupid face.

"I can't believe this! I've told you you've gotta knock! What are you doing here?"

He put his hands up. "Please, Lennina. Don't be like that. I've come in peace. Please don't be hostile."

"Hostile? I just want some privacy. Is that too much to ask?"

He bowed his head. "I've just come to talk. That's all."

I frowned. Apparently it was too much to ask. "I don't want to talk to you. Remember me getting a Restriction Order out against you? That RO is still in effect. I want you to leave."

"I can't do that. This Talent training is very important. Can't you see what we're doing here? What you learn and what you do with it will make a difference to the universe. It's not exactly the job you were after, but it's better than the job you had. You have a chance here to make a real difference. Our research here is so important. We could be helping to enhance the human race."

He was talking in circles.

"That might be true, but it has nothing to do with you and me. I can work with Xander and Dr Rowen without you being here."

He took a step forward. "Xander? Is he that trainer?"

"Yes. He is teaching me how to use my Talent."

His eyes darkened. "You like him, eh?"

"What? No! He's..." *a jerk...* "he's my trainer."

"Having to be discreet because of a professional relationship hasn't stopped you before."

"Are you serious right now? You're going to accuse me again? You're—" I stopped myself. Last time I'd called him crazy, I'd ended up with broken ribs.

"Lennina, darling. I hear what you're saying. But you must understand. I can't *not* feel jealous. It's not something that comes easily for me. Not after what happened. Not after what she did. Did I tell you I walked in on them?"

Yes. Many times.

"They were doing it right there — on *our* bed. It was so devastating. I don't know if I'll ever get over it."

"You're not the only person who's ever been cheated on, you know."

I pushed my ex-boyfriend's face out of my mind.

"Yes, but you need to understand how bad it was for me. To find them like that..."

"Look. You've told me all this before. It doesn't excuse what you did to me. You gave me a black eye and broke my ribs!"

"I admit I have some anger issues, but you need to understand that my father wasn't a good role model for me. He had anger issues and maybe they've rubbed off on me."

Not this again.

I did *not* want to hear it all again.

"I'll admit that I tell it like it is, but that's just me. I don't want to beat around the bush. If there's something I don't like, I'll just come right out and say it. You know that about me. But I can change. At least a bit. I can try. For you."

He stepped further into the room and tried to wrap his arms around me.

I pushed him away. "Stop it!"

"Lennina. Don't push me away. We're good together. We can be together again. I'll show you what I can do. I'll be everything you want me to be."

He put his arms around me and I couldn't move my arms. He tried to kiss me and I turned my head away.

"Lennina. Don't be stupid. You're being childish."

He grabbed my jaw with one hand and forced my face toward him as he pressed his lips to mine. Flashes of the night he'd assaulted me ran through my mind and all the horror came flooding back. I had to get out of here. NOW.

"LET ME GO!" I screamed into his mind.

An incredible heat built up with my anger and burst from me in a flash of light. Malvolio flew backwards through the air and hit the wall with a loud thump.

CHAPTER 19

I Need to Get Out. NOW!

I gasped as I looked down; Lightning danced over my fingertips.

I'd used my Lightning power on him.

I walked over to find him unconscious on the floor and noticed that where he'd hit the wall, there was a concealed door on the opposite side of my room from the bathroom. I hadn't noticed it there before.

My eyes widened. There was *another* place they could get in? It was unbelievable.

I looked down at Malvolio again. His clothes were charred where I'd hit him in the chest. Was he okay? Was he still alive?

I swallowed. What if I'd killed him?

I found a pulse on his neck and breathed a sigh of relief. The thought of me actually killing someone sent a chill down my spine.

Okay. I had to think. I had to get out of here. I would be in big trouble for zapping the MIC of Galaxy Mech.

The door swished open and Raynar rushed over to Malvolio's prone form. "What happened?"

"He deserved it."

"He needs medical attention," he said.

"I don't care."

I slipped out the door while Raynar was checking Malvolio for a pulse and ran down the hallway.

Raynar called after me, but I wasn't stopping for anyone.

I knew my way around a little better this time and I thought maybe I could zap anyone who got in my way. Or at least push them away from me.

As I slowed to a jog, I wished that one of my abilities was to teleport.

Then I could learn to master that skill and teleport both of us out of here in a blink.

But there was no use wishing. I'd have to use the abilities that I did have. It was ironic that they were teaching us the skills we'd need to escape.

I'd make them pay for what they were doing to us. The authorities would shut them down.

"Lennina? What's wrong?"

Daniel could probably sense the anger radiating from me, even from this distance. *"Daniel? Where are you?"*

"Just started training. What's going on?"

"Malvolio, that's what."

"What happened?"

"He—" I swallowed. *"He forced me to kiss him. He's such a bastard! I can't get away from him in here. I need to get out. NOW!"*

"Hey, are you alright?"

"Yeah. No. Kind of. I pushed him away and he hit the wall. I knocked him out. And I used my Lightning power on him."

"Really? Wow. Where are you now?"

I breezed past a woman in a green uniform. She stared after me, but didn't say anything. *"I'm headed for the doors. No one's gonna stop me this time. I zapped Malvolio's arse, so I'll zap anyone else that gets in my way. You coming?"*

"How am I gonna get away from Sarinda?"

"Lie to her. Knock her out if you have to. I'm outta here."

"Hang on. It didn't work last time. Can't we work something out here?"

"No! I gotta go before Malvolio does something worse than just kiss me. Rowen won't keep him away. No one can protect me. Not even you."

That probably hurt him, but it was the truth. I had no idea where he was or if they'd ever let us see each other again.

"I don't even know where you are," he said quietly.

"Hey, I know. I wasn't having a go at you. I know it's not your fault. But I've got to go. If you can't come with, I'll go it alone and get some help. Someone out there will sort this crap out. They can't keep us here

indefinitely."

"I know. Make sure you tell someone not related to The Company. They can send someone to investigate."

I ran past a man in a blue uniform. He turned and called for me to stop, but I kept going. I seriously needed to work out or something. I was out of breath already and I hadn't made it to the door yet.

"Where are you?"

"I'm nearly to the doors. I'm not stopping this time. I'll knock them all down."

"Be careful."

"I will. But I've got to do this."

I slowed down as I went around the last bend before the exit and peered around the corner. Six guys armed with stunners and dressed in black. So a lot more security than last time. I should've got it right the first time.

I ducked back around the corner and tested my ability to use the Lightning. I should have done that before now, but it was too late to worry about it.

I felt the heat from before and let it build up inside me. I was surprised it was still there and that it responded. I let out a small amount and marvelled at the Lightning that danced across the hall.

I readied myself. It would take a big blast to knock them all down at once, and I'd have to make it good if I wanted them to lose consciousness.

I had no idea what I was doing.

I took a deep breath and spun around the corner. Before they could react, I blasted them with Lightning and some telekinetic energy and they were flung back against the doorway, crumpling to the floor in a pile of arms and legs.

I was surprised at how well that had worked. I checked them; they were all unconscious.

As I picked my way through the bodies toward the door, movement caught my eye. I turned and flung some energy at the two men that were running my way, but hadn't had time to let it build up, so one of them went down and the other stumbled and kept running.

He pulled out his stunner and I flicked it out of his hand. He pulled out some other device and I flicked it away too. I couldn't make out what it was, but guessed it was some kind of weapon.

I blasted him into a wall and spun around, ready for anyone else who might run around the bend.

There was no one else, so I continued toward the door. I was almost there. Almost free.

"Lennina. What's going on?"

"I'm nearly there, Daniel. I'm—"

The blast hit me from behind and launched me into the door. I managed to put my arms up before I face-planted the metal, and fell on top of one of the men, twitching uncontrollably.

It stopped before Xander reached me and I pushed him away with a fairly weak blast. There wasn't time to gather the energy needed to knock him out.

I heard him hit the wall or floor and stumbled to my feet, but he was getting up too.

"Lennina?"

"Lenni, stop this now," Xander called. "It won't end well for you. You can't leave."

Lenni? Seriously? "I'm going and you're not going to stop me this time."

I was glad he'd stopped to talk so I could gather some energy — but he was probably doing the same.

"I'm gonna whoop your arse, girl. Just give it up now and save yourself some pain."

"No. I'm getting out of here."

"Fine, Lenni, have it your way."

"Stop calling me Lenni!"

We both let loose at the same time and the Lightning smashed together in mid-air with a deafening crack. The force of it pushed us both back; me into the door and Xander back a few paces.

I was trying to build up my energy as more people in black came around the corner.

Xander turned to look at them and I took the opportunity to blast him. He turned back to me as the Lightning hit him in the chest and he let out a shout.

The security guys raised their stunners. "Freeze!"

I pushed them away without using the Lightning and watched them tumble to the floor, but a moment later, something made me feel on edge, like I was shaking all over, but when I looked at my hands, they were steady. I didn't feel right.

What?

One of the security guys walked toward me and I could hardly move. I couldn't use my Talent. I couldn't feel the energy inside me. I couldn't blast him. What was happening to me?

He smirked and held up a small device in his hand. "What's the matter, freak? Can't use your Talent?"

It felt like my insides were vibrating and it made me nauseous. "What is that thing?"

"Something that stops you freaks from fryin' us with that Lightnin' shit."

The nausea welled up in my stomach. This couldn't be good.

The guards that were still conscious picked themselves up off the floor and retrieved their stunners. Before I could react, they were all pointing at me.

Xander moaned and I could tell the device was affecting him too. "Did you have to use that thing?" he asked.

The guy looked at him with the same smirk. "Yes. Us Normies have to protect ourselves somehow."

Normies?

Xander retched and the security guard jumped back, but somehow Xander held it in.

My stomach roiled at the thought and I turned to vomit all over the nearest wall. I tried not to get any on the men at my feet, even though they probably deserved it.

Xander moaned again. "Just stun her already so you can turn that thing off." The guard was enjoying this. "I'll report you to Rowen if you don't do as I say!"

That got his attention and he fired the stunner before I could even think to react.

Pain shot through me and I sank to the floor with every muscle convulsing. The blackness soon followed.

CHAPTER 20
Punished

I woke up to find that I was in a room that was completely flooded with light. The light was bright, even through my eyelids.

I struggled to remember what had happened. It came back to me in a flood. My disastrous escape attempt.

That's when the noise started. It sounded like white noise. Then over the top of that, I could make out a humming, droning noise that became louder than the white noise, drowning it out.

What was going on? Where was I?

The floor I was lying on was padded. That was weird.

The noise receded.

"Lennina." The voice was coming into the room via a speaker. It was Dr Rowen. I really hated that woman.

I squinted and shaded my eyes and could make out an empty room with white walls. "Where am I? What happened? What are you doing?"

"You are being punished. You and your partner cannot be allowed to continue hurting members of my staff. Mr Dermid and five others are in the Infirmary. You could have killed him."

I sat up. "Punished? What do you mean? What are you gonna do this time? Don't even think about hurting Daniel again."

"You will be taught a lesson."

"What? How? How long do I have to sit in here?"

No answer.

"What am I meant to be doing in here?"

Nothing.

Great.

That's when the noise became louder.

Maybe this was my punishment. Bright light and boring noise.

Punishment? More like torture. A chill ran down my spine. Torture. What else would they do to me?

This wasn't right. They couldn't do this. It was against Intergalactic Law. They couldn't keep us here indefinitely. They couldn't torture us.

I tried not to panic or let the light and noise annoy me because that's what they wanted. It was hard to keep calm.

There seemed to be something else now, underneath the noise. It made me feel on edge, and I recognised the horrible shaky feeling and the accompanying nausea.

Aw, hell no.

They were using that device on me again, as well as the other stuff?

How was I going to get through this? The shaky feeling was hard to endure by itself. I thought I would lose it if they left me in here too long. My anxiety rose.

No.

I wouldn't let them beat me. I would fight this.

I crawled over to the nearest wall and leaned my back against it. It was padded too. I assumed the padded room was so I couldn't hurt myself too much, but it irked me because people always associated a padded room with someone being insane. At least I wasn't in a straitjacket.

I pulled my legs up and wrapped my arms around my knees. I could do this. I *would* do this. I'd endure it for however long I'd be in here for. I just had to stay calm and not let it get to me.

I thought about things to distract myself. Adamo on his first day of school. Adamo learning to walk. Adamo falling over and crying, then picking himself up off the floor so he could toddle over to me for a hug.

I put my head down to block out the light as much as I could and kept playing happy memories over and over in my head.

I moved on to memorising the theories I'd learned in my studies, pretending I was studying for an assessment. I could do this.

I thought about when I left Azaeli to come here. My mother pretending she was okay with it, tears in her eyes. Adamo trying to be grown up and not cry. It didn't work for long. He gave me a huge hug and Mum joined in. I told them not to worry, that I'd call them regularly and come home between Rotations — that six months wasn't that long.

I'd told them it would be alright. But it wasn't alright. I had to drag my thoughts away from there. It wouldn't help me get through this nightmare.

Back to thoughts of baby Adamo. He was so cute when he was little.

The nausea increased. How could I get through it now?

I had to do it. I had to try. I didn't want to let them beat me.

A memory of my mum and dad talking and smiling at each other hit me. I hadn't thought about that day in so long. It was Adamo's third birthday and we were all so happy together. It was before everything went wrong. Before he left us.

There was no hint of what was to come. Nothing at all to indicate that he wasn't happy or that he wouldn't be around in a few months' time.

I couldn't understand how Mum could let us think he'd left with no reason behind it. Okay, so she didn't want to tell us when we were kids, but we were old enough now to understand and to keep quiet about it.

It was too late to worry about that now. I had to think about what to do with the information. I wondered if there was any way to get in contact with him to get his side of it. I was still angry with him though.

I pushed the memory away. I needed something positive to focus on.

My stomach roiled as I concentrated on Daniel's face in my mind. His green eyes and perfect smile. His dark hair and muscular arms. I remembered how it had felt to be in his arms. When he kissed me, the world around me melted away and all I could think of was him and how he made me feel.

My head pounded and my eyes ached.

How long have I been in here?

Bile rose in my throat.

How long do I have to put up with this?

The urge to vomit hit me hard and I turned to the side to avoid getting it all over me. I retched over and over until I was only bringing up bile. I stumbled away from the mess as tears ran down my cheeks.

How can they do this? Torture is illegal!

The noise became unbearable and the pain in my head reached a new level as the blackness engulfed me.

CHAPTER 21

That's Private!

When I came to, I was lying on a bed in the darkness. My stomach felt like it had turned itself inside out.

Once my eyes adjusted to the lack of light, I recognised my room.

My body ached all over and my brain buzzed and pounded. I still couldn't believe what they'd done. How could I ever get out of here?

I had a sudden urge to vomit and bolted out of bed and into the bathroom. I didn't have anything to bring up and retched repeatedly. My stomach muscles were aching by the time I finished and I stumbled back to bed as the tears came.

I couldn't remember ever feeling so sick.

I wanted to call Daniel, but didn't have the energy. I was positive my pounding head would make it impossible anyway.

I had to lie still for a long time before the pain died down enough for me to sleep.

If they thought I would give up on any ideas of escape after this, they were mistaken. This punishment wouldn't stop me. It made me more determined.

I was going to get out of here, or die trying.

———— ⋆·☆·⋆ ————

The day after my torture session, I was expected to go back to training like nothing had happened. I couldn't believe it. They didn't care about us at all.

I felt drained and hollow. Not just because of the 'punishment,' but because I didn't know how we were going to get out of this place. I couldn't go on like this.

Daniel was livid when I told him what they'd done to me. He'd felt what I was feeling up until they'd turned the device on and didn't know what had happened after that.

There was nothing we could do unless we escaped or got the word out somehow. Then Daniel's uncle would be able to help us with the legalities of it.

Daniel had been trying to find a way to escape from Sarinda when he felt the attack on me. He was able to run out of the room when Sarinda was affected by Xander's pain. But then was affected again when he'd felt my pain.

And of course Baudin was able to stop him.

I sat in the chair opposite Xander in the training room, scowling at him and at the whole universe, and he actually looked concerned. Like he actually cared. Or maybe I'd imagined it.

"Don't look at me like that. It's your own fault."

"You could have warned me about that device. It was horrible."

He leaned forward. "The destabiliser? That's your worst enemy. You need to learn to do as you're told and that you can't escape from here. You'll go home when we say you can, and not before."

I crossed my arms. "Surely you don't agree with them using that thing? It affected you too."

He sat back. "A necessary evil. To keep us in line."

"I thought you were the Golden Child and that you liked it here."

He crossed his arms too. "You're funny. I earned my position here as a trainer. I do like it here. That thing is for people like you who can't do what they're told." He cleared his throat. "So today I need to teach you how to block someone from your mind."

"What?" That was an abrupt change of subject. "I can already do that. You saw that for yourself."

"But you need to be able to defend yourself if someone ever gets past your wall. Once I was past it, I had free reign."

I cringed at the reminder. "Only because I was letting you in. I didn't try to keep you out."

"Exactly. That's why you have to do more training in that area."

This was not what I wanted, especially after the torture session I'd had, but maybe he was right. It was not a pleasant experience having him poking around in my head. I needed to learn how to kick him out. And anyone else, for that matter.

I sighed. "What do I have to do then?"

He smiled and a shiver ran down my spine. "You need to let me into your mind, past your outer wall, and I'll start poking around. You need to work out how to block me out of each place I try to access. It's a hard thing to explain how to do. The best way to learn is if you just do it."

My chest tightened. I didn't want to do this. It was bad enough last time. How was I going to let him do this without panicking?

I didn't want him to see my thoughts. They were personal. He had no right to see them, but I'd have to let him in in order to be able to kick him out.

I sucked in a breath. I could do this. After my supposed *punishment*, this should be easy.

"Okay."

We sat opposite each other and I struggled to let my wall down enough to let him in.

Once he was in my mind, he dove straight into my memories. I wasn't ready for that and suddenly I was pulled back into the past to a day I'd rather erase from my mind forever.

Daddy stood in the doorway carrying big suitcases.

I walked over slowly. "Daddy? Where are you going?"

He put them down on the floor. "Oh, Honey. I have to go away."

"But why?"

"It's hard to explain, but just remember that I love you and Mummy and Adamo."

I ran to him and wrapped my arms around his leg like I used to do when I was younger.

He tried to pull my arms off him. "No, Honey. Don't do that. I have to go now."

Adamo came wandering out of his room rubbing the sleep from his eyes. "Daddy?"

Daddy pulled harder and I let go. "No. I gotta go."

Mummy came out of her room and pulled me and Adamo into a hug. She was crying, which made me and Adamo start crying.

She looked up at Daddy and he didn't say anything. He just walked out and shut the door.

Mummy held us both and we all cried for a long time.

I pushed the memory away. Tears wet my cheeks. *"What are you doing? That's private!"*

CHAPTER 22
We're Stepping Up Your Training

"What are you doing? You're supposed to be trying to block me, not sitting there reliving the past."

"How am I supposed to do that? That was... I can't concentrate when I get thrust into a memory like that."

"You have to ignore the memory and push me out."

How could I do that? I didn't know how I was supposed to ignore something as heart-wrenching as the day my father left us.

Xander didn't seem to care. He pushed back into my memories and I had no defence.

Jace looked me up and down. "Don't you ever wear dresses?"

I frowned. "No. Not really. You know that."

"You should. Wearing pants all the time isn't very feminine. You look like one of my mates."

What brought this on? We'd been together for a couple of years and he hadn't had a problem with the way I dressed before.

He put his hands on his hips. "When we went to the end-of-year ball last year, you wore that red dress with the low neckline. It was so sexy."

I crossed my arms. "Yeah, but I can't wear something like that all the time. Dresses aren't practical."

I tried not to get upset. It was only a memory. Why did Xander have to pick the painful stuff?

"You didn't try to push me out. You're not even trying, Lennina."

And with that, he went in again.

As I walked through the university's gardens, I heard voices. One of them was Jace. My heart clenched. I didn't want to see him after he'd carelessly dumped me for no real reason. Tears stung my eyes. I was still feeling raw.

I turned away. I'd find another way to the dormitory.

"You shouldn't have." It was a female's voice. It sounded familiar.

"But I did," he said. "Nothing but the best for my honey bumpkin."

Honey bumpkin? Seriously?

"It's just so pretty," she breathed.

"Happy anniversary."

"I can't believe it's been six months already. I love you, Cuddle Bunny."

My insides froze. Six months? They'd been together for six months? But he'd only broken up with me a week ago.

"Stop it! I don't want to remember this!"

"Then stop me."

I wiped the tears from my cheeks. *"I don't know how!"*

"You didn't have any trouble blocking me that first time. Work it out."

"But I don't know how I did that."

"That's why I'm here pushing you. So you can work out what you did."

"Can we stop now?"

"No."

"I need to rest and to work out how I'm gonna do this."

There was a pause. *"Okay."*

He withdrew from my mind and I wanted to punch him in the face.

I was back in counselling the following day and was trying to call Allador while Lysander took notes. I'd tried to call him many times since he'd healed me to see if he was okay and was hoping he'd answer me by appearing in the room so it would scare the bejesus out of Lysander.

He put his Palm-pad aside and looked up. "So, can you tell me why you keep trying to escape?"

"I've told you. What they're doing here is illegal. They can't keep us here."

He leaned back. "Well, I think you've seen that they can."

I sighed. "That's not what I meant. I mean according to Intergalactic

Law, they can't."

"What have you got against Katoa?"

I leaned forward. "Are you serious? They are the people who are keeping us captive!"

Lysander squeezed the bridge of his nose. "They are keeping you here for training purposes. Nothing more. Nothing sinister."

"I don't think so. Do you know what they did to me? That was torture! They can't be allowed to do that to people. They need to be stopped."

"These are unique and unusual circumstances and they need a way to control people who have power that is way beyond those of normal humans. If we don't have some method of control, chaos will reign. Can you imagine if Talented people wandered around attacking people at random? We need to make sure that that doesn't happen."

A shiver went down my spine. "I'm not going to go around doing that."

"But you did."

"I was trying to get out of here and to defend myself!"

"And the next time you do something, you'll have an equally good excuse — at least in your mind."

"It's not like that. I'm not the bad guy here."

"Neither am I."

I huffed. "Coulda fooled me."

There was a pause and I tried to reach out to his mind. Maybe I could find out what was going on using telepathy. Lysander wouldn't tell me the truth. He would only tell me what The Company wants me to believe.

I couldn't get through. He had a mental shield in place. I'd been told that anyone could learn how to create a mental shield — not just the Talented. As far as I knew, Lysander wasn't a Talent, so it made sense for him to learn if he was a counsellor for a bunch of Telepaths.

He cleared his throat and steepled his hands. "So. How do you feel about your newfound power?"

"It's awesome, but it has caused me to be locked up in here."

He pushed his steepled hands closer together. "We've been over the reasons for you being here."

I leaned back in my chair. "Yeah, well. I've had enough."

Why was I even answering his dumb questions?

"Define awesome."

"You don't know what awesome means? And I thought you were an educated man."

"Lennina. I thought you were going to be serious today."

"You thought wrong. I'm not in the mood for serious."

"Why won't you take these sessions seriously?"

I counted off on my fingers. "I don't want to. I don't care. They are of no benefit."

"That's simply not true."

I glared at him.

"So—"

"Don't start every sentence with 'so.'"

"Does it bother you?"

"Yes."

"Okay. Tell me about the tunnel collapse."

"You haven't asked me about the alien or how I feel about it healing Daniel and I. Why is that, Doc?"

He faltered. "We will get to those questions at a later time."

"Sure we will. Don't you wanna know what they're like? How you can see right through them? How they communicate telepathically? How it feels when the warmth spreads through you and the pain disappears? I had three broken ribs and now I'm totally fine. It feels great, Doc, that's how it feels. But when I think about the fact that Daniel made First Contact with a previously unknown alien species on the planet and no one up here gives a shit, I think that maybe there's something more going on. Then add the fact that there's breathable air on Kronos and you've got a recipe for a really cool conspiracy theory."

"Oh, there is no conspiracy going on here, I can assure you."

"Can you? 'Cause I think that maybe I'm right."

"You didn't answer my question about how you feel about your abilities."

"Yeah. Pretty good avoidance tactic, don'tcha think?"

He sighed and it sounded almost like a growl. "I think we might wrap it up there, then. I will be seeing you again very soon, my dear."

"Good. Can I go now?"

"Yes."

I jumped out of my seat, waved a big, over-exaggerated goodbye at him, and strode out of the room.

I sighed as I made my way to the cafeteria, glad to be rid of the idiot counsellor. Pity I couldn't shake my guard dog too.

"Lennina. There you are."

I stopped walking, rolled my eyes and sighed again. Dr Rowen.

She walked right up to me. "I'd like to speak with you."

I turned to face her. "Yes?"

There was that fake smile I hated. "Please come with me."

But I was hungry. "Where to?" I tried to read her mind, but she had a solid shield in place too. I was disappointed, but not surprised.

"We're stepping up your training and there'll be some changes."

That didn't sound good. "Will it mean that I can go home sooner? Because I'm on board with that."

"That's up to you. Your attitude still leaves a lot to be desired, and your inability to take things seriously is affecting your progress."

I rolled my eyes again. I couldn't help it.

Why does everyone and their space rat have a problem with my damn attitude?

I reluctantly followed her to a random door that looked like all the others in this prison and she placed her hand on the scanner. The door opened and I followed her in.

I gasped. Daniel was standing near the doorway talking with a slim blonde woman.

CHAPTER 23

Hey, You

Daniel turned and smiled, his dark hair hanging down over his left eyebrow. *"Hey, you."*

My heart skipped a beat or two and felt like it had swelled to twice its normal size in my chest. I could hardly breathe and warmth spread through me. *"Hey, you."*

So much had happened since the last time I'd actually seen him. It had been so long and I'd felt like I would lose my sanity.

My legs didn't wait for me to decide what to do. I was walking over to him before I realised what I was doing.

Daniel stepped forward, arms out. *"Come here."*

My breath caught in my throat and I fell into his warm embrace.

The jolt of electricity from the Lightning Connection made me jump. I'd forgotten about it, but I relished the buzzing sensation that went with it.

I squeezed him tight. *"I can't believe you're really here."*

He stroked my hair and the buzz running through my entire body was blissful. *"Aww, did you miss me?"*

"You know I did."

I pushed my face into the crook of his neck and couldn't hold back the tears. All the things that had happened recently rushed through my mind and the memory of when he was trapped underground made me cry harder.

"Shhh. It's okay."

I let Daniel see in my mind what I was remembering and he held me tighter. I didn't know where the idea came from to share my memories like that. It seemed like a natural thing to do.

His hand made swirling motions across my shoulder blade and I revelled in the feeling. I concentrated on the motion and it helped to calm me.

I remembered we had an audience, but I was past caring. They already knew I was in love with Daniel; they knew we shared the Lightning Connection.

Someone cleared their throat, but I ignored them.

Dr Rowen spoke up. "Alright, break it up."

No!

I held him tighter.

"Break it up, or I'll separate you again."

That got my attention. We slowly turned toward her, still giving each other a one-armed hug.

It looked like there was something sour in her mouth. "This is Sarinda Markin, one of our trainers here at Katoa." Rowen gestured to the slim blonde woman who'd been talking to Daniel. "She has been training Mr Javolo and will be involved in part of your training as well."

I said a quiet "hello" and Sarinda gave a curt nod.

Rowen continued, "From now on, your training will involve both of you doing activities together."

Good. It's about time. "I don't understand why you kept us apart in the first place if we're supposed to be Connected," I said.

"It was part of our studies. We needed to see how you fared separately, and now we can observe your progress as you work together."

That's the only reason we were separated? I wanted to slap her face.

I was surprised at myself for how often I felt like hitting someone lately. I'd never been like this before, but these people were making me so frustrated and angry.

Daniel ran his free hand through his hair. "So what happens now? What kind of training are you talking about?"

The fake smile was back. "We will get you to train together to see how much you improve. Our studies have shown that there is an increase in power once the partners are together once again."

That was interesting. And it could come in handy for my next escape attempt. Because there *would* be a next one.

Daniel made little circular patterns on my back again and I tried not to get distracted by it. "When do we start?"

"Tomorrow morning. You will be shown to your new training room." She nodded. "That will be all for now."

It seemed that we were dismissed and we couldn't get out of there fast enough.

Daniel took my hand while we walked through the halls and I concentrated on the buzz that ran through me as I tried to ignore the guards trailing behind us. I was still in shock. It had been so long since we'd been allowed to see each other and I was beginning to think I'd never see him again.

"Hey," he said as he squeezed my hand. *"It's so good to see you!"*

I smiled and squeezed back. *"Yes. You too. I can't believe how long they've kept us apart."*

"Me neither." He turned to me. *"Where can we go that's a bit more private?"*

I looked around and recognised where we were. *"We're not too far from my room, so we could go there, I guess."*

His smile turned wicked. "Oh, *hell* yeah!"

I realised what I'd just said and how it sounded, which made my cheeks flush. "Oh, um... I mean... I didn't mean... I meant, just to talk and..."

He winked at me, which made him look so sexy. *"I knew what you meant. I couldn't resist."*

"Don't be mean."

He put a hand to his heart. *"Who, me? Never."*

I giggled. Five minutes with Daniel and my spirits were already lifted. We rounded the bend and I headed for my door.

Daniel stopped. "Wait a minute — that's my room!"

He was pointing at the door further down from mine.

"Are you serious?"

"Yes."

"Are you sure? All these corridors look the same."

"Yes."

I looked at the distance between the doors. His room would have to be the room on the other side of my bathroom.

Surely I hadn't been next to Daniel this whole time? My blood boiled thinking about it.

Maybe they thought it was funny. "I can't believe they did this!"

"They are such arseholes."

I ran a hand through my hair. *"I have a locked door in my bathroom. Don't tell me you've been on the other side of it this whole time!"*

"It looks like it. I have a bathroom on the opposite side of my room, but I noticed a door on the other side — right where your bathroom is — that is always locked."

I had to check it out for myself. I went in and went straight to the door in the bathroom, which opened to show Daniel's room. When we checked, the door to his bathroom was now locked. What the hell was going on?

"Not only are they letting us see each other, but they want us to share a bathroom as well?"

I couldn't help the smile spreading across my face, but I was kinda dumbfounded after we'd been kept apart for so long.

Daniel turned to me and put his arms out. I didn't hesitate and fell into his embrace. I welcomed the Lightning jolt and tingling sensations, closed my eyes and soaked him in. This is what I'd been dying to do for nearly two weeks, but it had seemed so much longer.

I breathed deeply and inhaled his scent. That woodsy aroma that I remembered from the last time I was in his arms brought back pleasant memories.

A few tears leaked out. I was happier than I'd been in a long time. Daniel stroked my hair and I squeezed him tighter.

"I missed you," he said.

"I missed you too."

My brain was still reeling, not believing that this was real. I pulled away so I could see his face. Before I could even think about it, I leaned forward and kissed him on the lips. He froze for a second, then relaxed and pulled me closer.

It was just small kisses at first, but then they became longer and more urgent. I became lost in him and the world fell away. There was nothing else. I couldn't get enough of him and it seemed like I couldn't hold him close enough.

We finally stopped for a breath and held each other tight.

"Wow," Daniel finally said. *"That was amazing."*

I smiled.

I thought about all the training and torture and other crap we'd been through. If we had more of it to come, being together would definitely make it easier to cope. *"I didn't think they'd ever let me see you again."*

"I was getting pretty bloody worried too."

We sat on his bed and I had to say what was on my mind. *"Why have they let us share a bathroom? Not that I'm complaining, but they wouldn't be doing it just because they're being nice."*

Daniel ran a hand through his hair. *"I know. It's not their style. I guess it's the next step in their 'studies,' but I don't like being the subject of their experimentation. It's like we're not people anymore."*

The buzzing sensations ran up and down my arms. *"Yeah."* I sighed. *"But I don't think I can deal with this anymore. I can't keep going like this."*

"You got this. You can do it. But you need to stop trying to escape."

CHAPTER 24
He Didn't Deserve You

My eyes snapped to his. *"What? I can't do that."* My heart pounded. *"You mean you wanna stay here?"*

His eyebrows shot up. *"No, of course not. I'm saying that we need a plan. I keep telling you that."*

"I know. It's just... things keep happening."

"Malvolio. I know. They should've locked him up after what he did to you, not bow down to his every command. He's nothing but a lowlife scum and an arsehole and he didn't deserve you."

His words moved me. I didn't want the tears to fall, but two big drops ran down my cheeks and dripped onto my chest. *"Thank you."*

His eyebrows drew together. *"For what? Insulting him?"*

I smiled through my tears. *"No. For caring."*

A grin crept across his face. *"Anytime."*

I hugged him and savoured the feeling of being in his arms. I shivered as he stroked my hair.

"We need to get out of here and not *get caught,"* he said. *"We need to look at options. There has to be a way to sneak out."*

I ran a hand down his muscular back as I thought about what we could do. *"Dress as staff of some kind and walk out? Or hide inside something they're taking out of here?"*

"We could go down the laundry chute."

I pulled back enough to see his face. *"Or the garbage chute."*

A frown creased his brow. *"No. I'm not sure what they do with the garbage here. We could get crushed or incinerated, or maybe dumped out of an airlock."*

I shuddered. *"Knowing Katoa, it's probably all three."*

"If we dressed as staff members, we'd need a way to get our hands on some suitable clothes. Nurses' uniforms or some security gear."

"Yeah. Cleaners, maybe?"

He rubbed his jaw. *"You might have something there. There should be some service corridors inside the walls. If we could get in there..."*

"Yes. We could go anywhere on the station. That sounds like a good idea."

He held me a little tighter. *"We'll start looking for possible entries to the service corridors wherever we go. Hopefully, they're marked."*

I leaned my head on his chest and smiled. We'd find a way out of here.

My stomach chose that moment to let me know it wanted to be fed and I was embarrassed by how loud it was.

"I guess we should go and get something to eat," Daniel said. "Before you waste away."

I smiled. "Let's go."

He took my hand as we walked and it made me feel warm inside. Our guards followed along behind.

There were a few stares from the staff members in the cafeteria, but we were left alone to eat. We couldn't stop staring at each other, so the other people around us didn't matter.

We ate quickly and talked about our plan.

"I think I know where there's a door," Daniel said. *"Over near Lysander's office. I'll have a better look next time I'm there."*

I tried to picture the hallway in my mind. I hadn't paid attention to the other doors. *I should pay more attention to my surroundings in here.*

Once we'd finished, Daniel stood. "Let's go."

I couldn't wait to get back to my room. Back to some semblance of privacy.

Maybe.

Probably not.

"We need to be careful in case there's cameras in our rooms," I said.

"Yeah. Probably. We should assume that they're watching us, then we won't do something we don't want them to see."

We went in through my door and sat on my bed together.

I kept thinking of him as Daniel and not Javolo. My brain still had a hard time accepting it. I thought of all the times we'd talked and laughed together; his scratchy voice over the Com. Here he was. But my mind kept telling me this was the guy I met at the restaurant that day.

I couldn't put them together. I played conversations I'd had with Javolo over in my mind as if they were recorded on a disc. Then conversations with Daniel.

He gave me a lopsided grin. "What?"

I couldn't help smiling back at him. "Nothing."

His grin turned into a full smile that showed his teeth. "It's not nothing. What is it?"

My cheeks warmed. *"I'm having trouble picturing you as Javolo..."*

He laughed and I wondered what was funny. Was he making fun of me? This was so not funny.

"I'm having the same trouble," he admitted. *"My mind can't get around it. Lennina Callista... It won't sink in, no matter what I tell it."*

I was glad I wasn't the only one. *"I was so shocked when I heard your full name on the Vid. And when the other channel had your face up on the screen too, it was surreal. I don't know if I would've worked it out on my own..."*

"You're a smart girl. It would've come to you. Sooner or later. Plus, I was gonna tell you, remember?"

"Yeah."

We laughed. It was good to laugh after everything we'd been through in here.

We sat for a while in silence and I tried to relax. He was looking at me with a slight smile on his lips and I was sure that he was totally unaware of how gorgeous he was. I couldn't believe I had such intense feelings for him. My thoughts returned to the moments when I thought I'd lost him. My chest tightened and tears stung my eyes. It came out of nowhere and I was unable to stop it.

Daniel's eyes widened. *"What is it? What's wrong, Cal?"*

I didn't miss the fact that he'd called me by my nickname. "N-nothi ng..."

The floodgates opened and I turned so I could fall into his arms. I gasped at the jolt from our Connection, but the buzz was a comfort.

He pulled me close to him gently and stroked my hair. At first I couldn't talk, but I forced the words out. "Y-you nearly died..."

CHAPTER 25
Together

He hugged me tighter. "Shhh. It's alright. I'm here now and I'm not going anywhere."

Once I pulled myself together, I pulled back so I could see Daniel's face. His eyes were full of genuine concern.

"I'm sorry," I said.

He wiped my tears away gently with his thumbs. "For what? There's no need to apologise."

I tried to smile. *"It's just... I'm not a crier. It's... Everything is just too much, you know?"*

"Yeah. I know. I understand. But we're gonna get through it. Together."

I managed a smile at that. *"Thank you. You make it easier to deal with everything."*

He wrapped his arms around me once again and we stayed like that for a long time.

Daniel shook his head slowly and smiled at me.

"What?"

"That day, when I told you I'd seen the most beautiful woman I'd ever seen... and it was you all along..."

He shook his head again. My cheeks warmed. Tears formed, but these were happy tears. *"Thank you for the compliment..."*

Daniel leaned closer, deadly serious. *"You know, I wasn't just saying it."*

I squirmed in my seat. *"Yeah, sure. You—"*

"No, I'm serious. I really *meant* it. You really *are* the most beautiful woman I've ever seen." The heat in my cheeks flared and the blush spread to my throat and chest. I didn't know what to say. I wasn't used to having someone tell me I was beautiful. "And those blue eyes..." Daniel leaned even closer and took my hand in both of his, causing a little shock to travel up my arm and making me gasp. He apologised, but he didn't let go. "And the best thing is, you don't even know how beautiful you are."

I didn't know what to say to that.

"The most beautiful people in the world are the ones that don't know it. I love the way you blush when I tell you how beautiful you really are."

There was less than twenty centimetres between us. My heart pounded faster. He brought my hand to his lips and kissed it lightly. His lips were so soft and warm against my skin and the electricity hummed.

He kissed my hand again, this time, his lips lingered and sent a thrill through me.

He thought I was beautiful.

Don't cry! I told myself.

Too late.

Silent tears rolled down my cheeks and he squeezed my hand lightly.

"Hey, it's alright..." He put his arms out. "Come here."

The moment he took me into his arms, a sense of relief and warmth mixed in with the electricity. I melted into him and we held each other close. There was a feeling of longing, of needing each other and belonging together.

He rubbed my back. *"Hey. I didn't tell you to make you cry... It's just the truth."*

I found myself pulling him closer, holding him tighter. I was soaking it all up. The way he smelled. His warm body. His heartbeat. His strong arms wrapped firmly around me. His fingers tracing patterns absentmindedly on my back.

"I'm not sad. You make me so happy."

He sighed.

We stayed like that for a while longer, but then he pulled away a bit.

"I'd love to keep holding you like this. I would also like to keep talking and trying to make sense of this whole mess, but I think we both need to get some sleep."

My first thought was to tell him no. The last thing I wanted was to let him go. But he was right. And I was tired. *"Yes. You're right,"* I sniffed.

He placed his hands on my upper arms, rubbing gently and causing mild sparks. *"We can talk more tomorrow."*

I looked at my buzzing arms, then up at him and forced a smile. I did a double-take; I could actually *see* the sparks I was feeling, running along my arms and his fingers. "Whoah!"

"This is so spaced," he said as he kept rubbing.

It was amazing to watch.

Then I remembered we were supposed to be going to sleep. *"Okay. We'll talk more tomorrow."*

I didn't want him to let go. He dropped his arms slowly, reluctantly. Panic rose within me; I didn't want to be alone.

He smiled at me. *"Hey. I'm not going anywhere."*

Relief flooded through me.

I headed for the bathroom and got myself organised for bed, then it was Daniel's turn. When he came out and walked into my bedroom, I sucked in a breath. He was only wearing pyjama bottoms. And they were riding low on his hips.

His skin was completely flawless, thanks to Allador's healing ability, and well-muscled, thanks to his profession. The Mech-suit might be all hydraulics, but it still took some strength to operate it and do all that digging. And it showed.

His muscles flexed when he moved. His abs were ripped and there was a little trail of hair from his navel that disappeared under the waistband of his pants.

I forced myself to close my mouth and look at his face. The corner of his mouth twitched. He knew what I was gaping at. *"Like what you see?"*

My mouth fell back open and my cheeks flamed.

He smirked. *"I knew it."*

"Knew what?"

He chuckled. *"Remember I said you were secretly in love with me?"*

"I was *not*— Oh, I guess I was..."

He strode toward me. *"Yep. You just couldn't resist my charms."*

I rolled my eyes. *"Yeah, right."*

"It was such a deep dark secret that you *didn't even know it,"* he chuckled again.

This was more like a conversation we'd have over the Com. Maybe things wouldn't be weird after all.

Daniel approached me, his expression serious. *"Well, I guess we should get some sleep. I won't be far away. I'll just be out there in the other room, okay?"*

"No!" The thought of him not being close to me was too much to bear.

His eyebrows rose. *"You want me to stay in here?"* He smiled warmly, but then his eyebrows drew together. *"Are you sure?"*

How could I explain it when I didn't even understand it myself?

"I... I need *you close to me,"* I told him. *"I don't know why. I had this... need to see you when we were in the Infirmary. And it hasn't really gone away. It was totally overwhelming. I can't explain it. I lost my temper when they wouldn't let me see you. I don't know what's wrong with me. I feel this pull toward you..."*

Why did I tell him that? Way to scare him away. He would think I was overly-possessive.

"Hey," he said gently. I looked up at him. *"I... kinda feel like that too. I demanded that they let me see you, but it didn't change their minds. They even posted a guard at my door in the Infirmary so I couldn't sneak out and find you."*

So he'd felt the same way. *"I, uh, don't think it's normal. I guess it's part of what Xander was talking about with the Lightning Connection thing."*

He gave me half a grin. *"Yeah, maybe."*

"So, can you stay in here with me? I mean— I don't mean... I need to sort my head out... But..." I shuddered. *"I need you to... can you hold me close? I don't want to be alone..."* Tears stung my eyes at the thought.

He smiled again. *"Okay."*

"Really?"

"Really."

My heartbeat raced. He looked incredible smiling at me like that.

Was I insane? Asking a guy to lie in my bed with me and hold me close through the night and not do anything else? And him having no shirt on? Could I trust him to do that and nothing else? And could I trust myself? What if he expected more from me? What would I do?

I could always zap his arse...

I looked into his eyes. *"Does that sound silly — not wanting to be alone?"*

His face was serious, but sincere. *"No, of course not."*

I squirmed. *"But... I'm not ready for... anything more... I just need you to hold me..."*

He stepped closer. *"It's okay. I understand. Really. I do. I won't do anything you don't want me to do."*

"I'm not trying to mess with you," I said quickly. *"It's just that my head is all over the place... still trying to work it all out..."*

"Mine too..." Daniel stepped forward again. He reached out a hand to touch my forehead and suddenly there was a flash of Malvolio punching me in the face, and I put my hand up to fend him off as I stepped back.

Chapter 26
What the Hell Did He Do to You?

Daniel jumped back too. *"What happened? Did I hurt you somehow?"*

I covered my face with both hands. "No." It was barely a whisper. I felt incredibly stupid.

"Then, what is it?"

I lowered my hands and looked at him. His face was pale. What *did* just happen? Why did an image of Malvolio flash into my mind like that? Now Daniel thought that he'd hurt me.

"You didn't hurt me. It's just... I saw a flash of Malvolio in my mind... when he hit me..."

Daniel's face hardened and I sensed anger radiating from him, even as he pulled me in for a hug. *"Fuck!* What the *hell* did he do to you?"

I cringed inside as tears flowed freely down my cheeks and the buzz filled my body. Malvolio had done more than just hit me. More than just broken my ribs. Maybe I should have seen a counsellor back then. A real one. It had affected me more than I thought.

The vision of Malvolio had come from out of nowhere. I couldn't explain it. It wasn't like Daniel had swung his arm like he was going to strike me.

"I'm not scared you're going to hurt me. I... I don't know why I reacted like that."

"I know." Daniel simply wrapped his arms tighter around me and held me close. The buzz of our Connection combined with his touch made me feel safe. My fears melted away. He kissed the top of my head and I sighed.

Daniel picked me up carefully and carried me to the bed with my cheek against his bare chest. He sat down with me on his lap and rocked me gently and said things to reassure me, though they were soon lost as I thought about Malvolio.

Malvolio had ruined everything. He'd messed with my mind by being so manipulative, and then he'd turned on me. I'd been thinking that I was happy and in love, then it all turned sour. The man I thought I might even *marry* one day had almost knocked me out. Maybe he *did* knock me out — I wasn't sure. And to top it all off, had *kicked* me while I was lying there on the floor. That was no momentary loss of control. It wasn't a man lashing out in anger, then feeling remorse afterward. He'd had time to think after I'd hit the floor. The kick was malicious and meant to cause damage.

I was so stupid... so naive...

And all the put-downs before that... He belittled me and told all our friends that he'd found me and saved me from the gutter. I *wasn't* in the gutter. Being a Nav Operator was far from it. He was such an arrogant pig.

He'd insisted I resign from The Company at one point and move in with him so he could provide for me and care for me. He was *incapable* of caring for me. He didn't know how to love. I knew that now. What he really wanted was more control. I was his trophy girlfriend. And he could keep a better eye on me if we lived together. I shuddered at the thought. He used to call me several times a day as it was...

I used to tell Daniel about how Malvolio and I had gone here, there and everywhere together, but Daniel had already fallen for me. It must have been hard for him... Even that was messing with my head.

I knew I had to somehow get past it all and get on with a normal life with someone who actually cared for me. But I wasn't sure how I was going to do it...

What was it about Daniel that made me let my guard down? Especially so soon after Malvolio had beaten me. Maybe I could just see that Daniel was a good person. Maybe it had something to do with the Lightning Connection we shared. I held him tighter and he stroked my hair.

"I was torn," Daniel began, *"because I wanted what I couldn't have. But I couldn't tell you. I would never have forgiven myself if you lost your job and your career over me. Then, of course, I didn't know if you*

would ever see me as anything more than a friend..."

Why hadn't I realised that what I felt for him had changed to something more? Probably because I wasn't allowed to go there. Company rules.

It might have taken me a while to think things over if Daniel had come out and told me how he felt, but I probably would've come to the same conclusion; that Malvolio wasn't the one for me and what I felt for Daniel was actually way outside the Friend Zone I'd put him in.

"Then stupid What's-his-name came on the scene and I didn't want to interfere or ruin what could of been THE relationship for you. You seemed so happy and so in love, and it was hard to listen to you telling me all about it. But, you know, I just wanted you to be happy..."

I opened my mouth to speak, but didn't know what to say. My eyes stung, threatening tears.

"It would of been painful for me if you'd planned to marry him," he continued, *"but I thought I'd keep quiet and let it happen if it was what you really wanted..."*

He looked away for a few moments, trying to get his emotions under control, then looked back again and gave me a watery smile.

"Wait. You loved me before I met Malvolio?"

CHAPTER 27
You're Safe with Me

"Uh, yeah."

I gritted my teeth. *"Damn The Company and their stupid rules! If you could've told me — if you were allowed to tell me — I wouldn't have even* looked *at Malvolio..."*

"Well, damn..."

He leaned closer, causing a flutter in my stomach. I smiled up at him and he kept moving forward until our noses almost touched. I closed the gap and our lips met. Sparks flew and my eyes fluttered shut. The electricity made his touch all the more special. All the more intense. And his lips were so soft against mine.

He kissed me again. Just a feathery touch. I felt like I was going to melt.

He pulled away and smiled. *"You really are sooo beautiful,"* he breathed.

I melted.

His face was only centimetres from mine and he paused for a few seconds. I held my breath. He kissed me again and my heart sped up again. His tongue darted out and I nearly came undone. Why did him doing that feel so good? I let him push his tongue further into my mouth and felt like I was losing control. My arms were around him, pulling him closer. I couldn't get enough of him.

Malvolio's kisses had been nice and he'd made me feel special — at least at first — but it didn't have the intensity that I felt now. There was so much emotion wrapped up with Daniel's kisses.

What was I doing thinking about Malvolio now?

Daniel ran a hand down the centre of my spine and all thoughts of

Malvolio fled my mind. I concentrated on the present and let the heat swirl through me as I tried to get closer to Daniel. There was only him. Only us.

My heart was racing and it was too hot in the room. I needed to get even closer. I wanted to keep kissing him and I wanted to feel his strong arms around me, but he slowed things down and just held me close.

I breathed deeply and relaxed. A wave of exhaustion hit me and I knew we needed to sleep.

He loosened his hold. *"Hey. You need to rest. We'll talk more tomorrow."*

But I didn't want to sleep. I wanted to kiss him till the sun came up.

Daniel lowered me to the bed and pulled the blankets over me. He kissed my forehead and climbed into the other side of the bed and I became uneasy. Would he honour my request, or would he want more from me?

Daniel rolled onto his side and snuggled up, drawing me close to him. "Is this okay?"

My heart was pounding. *"Yes."*

"Tell me if I'm overstepping, okay?" His breath tickled my neck.

I wouldn't be able to sleep with him doing that, but I didn't want him to move away.

"Yes. I will. But you're not."

I felt like I needed to suck in big gulps of air, but I tried to breathe normally.

My heart wouldn't slow down. Why did I want him here with me? There was no way I could sleep with him so close.

I always slept on my side, so I knew I'd have to roll over if I wanted to get some sleep. It would be impossible to sleep if I turned to face him, which meant I'd have to roll away from him. *"Umm, I have to roll over,"* I told him. *"Don't take offence. It's just that I won't be able to sleep if I don't."*

"Hey. Do what you need to do to be comfortable. I won't be upset."

I smiled. *"Thank you."* I kissed him, then rolled over and he moved up behind me, spooning me.

He put his arm around me and rested his hand on the mattress. I smiled again. I let his limited embrace warm me right through to the core. Right into my very soul. He gave me a few gentle kisses on the back of my shoulder through my night shirt, which sent little tingles down my spine, then gave the command for the lights to turn off.

"Goodnight, Lennina Callista," he whispered.

"Goodnight, Daniel Javolo." I closed my eyes and my heart swelled. I couldn't help smiling to myself.

It was still weird putting both names together. Maybe if I kept saying it, it might make it easier to get it right in my head. I repeated it a few more times.

My mind raced, even though I needed to sleep.

I could hear his slow even breaths. Could feel his chest rise and fall. I'd been in a man's arms before, but this was different. This was someone who actually cared. And I really had to stop comparing the two situations. I had to shove Malvolio out of my head, my heart and my life. Forever.

I wished I didn't have him in my life right now.

Memories of so many conversations with Javolo rolled through my mind. We'd shared so much in between my instructions and his replies while finding and digging out the Amakio. He'd told me about his life as he grew up on Taon in a small town called Galina. And I'd told him what my life was like growing up on Azaeli.

We knew each other's likes and dislikes. There were funny situations and plenty of laughs, as well as plenty of lectures from my superiors. I hadn't cared. Daniel had endured the same lectures and he didn't give a damn either, because it didn't change things. We still talked and joked. It was fun to defy the supervisors, but I knew the only reason we hadn't been separated was because of the amount of Amakio we brought in every day.

My thoughts turned to the day we met. I'd been so angry with him for causing me to fall — I'd been in enough pain already. But I soon realised that I'd found someone who genuinely cared about me and the anger had faded. Now I knew why we'd gotten along so well and talked so easily — we already knew each other... If only I'd known who he was...

No point in thinking about that now. I needed to concentrate on the here and now. We were together and no one could tear us apart. They could separate us again, but we were one now. He loved me. I thought about how I felt about him and the feeling grew until it spread right through my heart and my body.

I felt so completely happy for the first time in my life, and finally drifted off to sleep with him wrapped around me.

——— ★·☆·* ———

I walked along, feeling dirt under my bare feet. This was wrong. I should be on solid flooring on the space station. How did I get here?

As I reached a bend in the tunnel I was now walking through, I could see that it was blocked off by rocks and soil. There was no way through.

The feeling of being trapped overwhelmed me. I couldn't breathe. I had to get out. I turned and ran the other way, but no matter how far I ran, I couldn't find the way out.

I looked ahead and noticed something underneath a large boulder. I slowed my steps. I crept closer.

It looked like a person...

No...

I didn't want to look, but I knew I had to.

No...

The person's legs were pinned under the rock. When I looked at the face, it was Daniel, staring up at nothing.

"Noooo!"

I woke up and I was actually crying. It was awful to see Daniel like that. I knew it was only a dream, but it was so realistic. I didn't know what I would do if I actually lost him for real.

I realised I wasn't in my own bed at home. I opened my eyes and tried to work out where I was.

Katoa Labs.

My heart sank. I'd forgotten. I tried to relax and wiped the tears away with the back of my hand. I rolled over onto my back and gave a start; there was a man lying next to me with his bare back to me. I jerked away toward the edge of the bed, my heart pounding.

The man gave a start and rolled over toward me and I flinched. It took a second or two to realise it was Daniel. His eyebrows shot up and he reached for me, then let his hand drop. "Hey, Cal. It's okay. It's me."

I couldn't believe I'd reacted like that. I was seriously messed up.

"Are you okay?"

"Yeah," I replied. Who was I kidding? "No. I forgot where I was and when I saw you, I freaked out."

"I'm sorry. It's okay. You're safe with me." He reached out a hand to me. "Come here."

I hesitated for a moment, trying to calm my racing heart and slow my breathing. I eased myself closer to him and he cupped my cheek. I welcomed the jolt of Lightning that came with his gentle touch and closed my eyes for a few moments, leaning into his hand. I needed his touch with the nightmare still fresh in my mind.

"The last thing I wanted to do was scare you," he said. "I wish I could help you."

"You already have."

My gaze travelled down to his bare chest. There were light creases on his skin from the sheets and I smiled despite the tears on my cheeks.

He frowned. "Why the tears?"

"Um, I was dreaming about being trapped underground and I found... You were trapped under some rocks and you were dead. It was so real... and when I woke up, I was actually crying." I was embarrassed. And still a little shaky. It had felt as real as when he'd run out of air and I'd thought he was dead.

He pulled me closer and I tingled all over. "It's okay. I'm here. I'm okay. I'm not going anywhere." He kissed me gently on the lips. "Good morning, Cal."

I couldn't stop the smile spreading across my face. "Good morning."

I was hyper-aware of the fact that he still had no shirt on. He kissed me again, long and slow. My arms automatically wrapped themselves around his neck and he deepened the kiss.

My heart raced as I slid a hand down his back. I felt his hard muscles across his chest and abs while his hand travelled over my back and down to my hip. He sighed against my lips as my fingers swept across his skin.

I marvelled at how it felt. I was fascinated. Each muscle flexed as he moved.

We broke apart to catch our breath and he wrapped his strong arms around me. I closed my eyes and leaned my head on his shoulder.

I couldn't believe he was here with me after the idiot doctors kept us separated for so long and after I thought I'd lost him.

There were no words to express how much gratitude I felt toward Allador for healing him. For healing me too, of course, but my injuries were nothing in comparison.

The Ampari had an incredible gift. Imagine being able to heal any injuries with just a touch. And no one had even known they existed.

It was easy to understand how The Company had failed to see there was a sentient race on Kronos during their preliminary scans and surveys. They didn't register as lifeforms.

They still hadn't picked up on the fact that they were not alone on the planet when they built the station and started mining. The Diggers eventually reported seeing them, but no one believed them. They believed those guys were suffering from some kind of mental breakdown.

The energy emitted by the Amakio was the reason The Company had travelled so far out into space to mine the mineral. It had some interesting properties and seemed to emit pure energy without heat. The Ampari actually fed off the energy to survive.

I was sure now that Katoa had found out about the Ampari and kept it quiet because the discovery of a sentient race would put an end to all mining on Kronos.

"We need to keep telling everyone that the Ampari are real and that they're intelligent," I said. *"The Company can't continue to mine here without their permission."*

Daniel played with my hair, twirling a lock around his fingers. *"Yes. The law is clear. We need to contact Starfleet Federation as soon as we're out of here."*

I nodded. I wished there was a way to get the word out while we were stuck in here.

Daniel slowly pulled away from me and sat on the edge of the bed. *"We need to get up."*

I couldn't take my eyes off his muscular back and marvelled at his fair skin — he wouldn't have had exposure to much sun underneath the surface of Kronos. He stretched out his arms and I watched the muscles bunch up on his shoulders and biceps.

He looked over his shoulder at me and smiled. *"Are you checkin' me out?"*

My cheeks flushed and I couldn't stop the smile spreading across my face. I'd been busted. Again.

"Well, who wouldn't want a piece of me? I'm just so awesome!"

I swatted his arm playfully. *"You really do have an ego problem, you know that? Some days it was so big I could see it on my radar screen."*

He laughed at that. *"Are you sure it was my ego you were seeing?"*

I tried to throw a pillow at his face, but I drew my arm back too far and my fingers hit the wall.

"Ow!"

The pillow still hit its mark, so I was happy about that.

He batted it away and frowned. *"Careful. Don't hurt yourself."*

I nursed my sore fingers. *"But it was worth it and you deserved it."*

Of course we couldn't have any time off to just enjoy each other's company. It was back to training in the dull little room with Xander trying to explain the best way to keep your concentration while holding a telepathic conversation and lifting something with your mind simultaneously. He'd already explained it to me before so I decided to try to read his mind while he was preoccupied.

I concentrated on his mind. He kept talking. I tried to go past the words he was saying and get to what was behind.

Nothing.

I tried again.

Nothing.

His mental shield was firmly in place.

I sighed. I might have been able to get through it if I pushed hard, but then he'd know I was there.

He looked at me with a strange expression. "Are you trying to get into my head? Without my permission? You know the rules, Lenni—"

"Don't call me Lenni!"

"—and you need to follow them."

I scowled at him. I'd have to be more careful. I needed to find out how much was too much poking around before someone noticed.

I had to change the subject. The possibility of the people at Katoa watching our every move had been on my mind all morning, so I thought I'd ask. "Are there cameras in our rooms?"

"Of course there are. There are cameras everywhere. They need to keep an eye on us. Make sure we're being good little trainees." He looked me in the eye. *"But, you know, they do have some sense of decency. Sort of. There are no cameras in the bathrooms, if you know what I mean."* And he winked at me.

What? Oh.

So, if we wanted privacy, we could go into the bathroom.

"Yeah. How do you think Sarinda got knocked up?"

They did it in the bathroom? Geez. "Sarinda is pregnant?"

He smiled. "Yep." He let the 'p' pop. *"I'm gonna be a daddy."*

CHAPTER 28

Newest Recruits

My stomach churned. *"Are you serious? How can you be happy about it?"*

His eyebrows came together. *"What do you mean?"*

"We're stuck here being part of their stupid experiments and you're gonna bring a baby into the universe? Are you crazy? What — is the baby gonna live here in Katoa Labs its whole life?"

"Heeyy. Keep ya shipsuit on. We're not going to be here forever."

"Aren't we?"

"Of course not. They'll finish up their studies sooner or later, and with all our training — that we get for free — *we can do something with our lives. Get decent careers. Make lots of credits. It'll be good. You'll see."*

"You keep telling yourself that. I won't believe it till I see it."

"They can't keep us here forever. That would be illegal."

I laughed out loud. *"You don't think that what they're doing here is illegal? They* tortured *me!"*

"You gotta stop trying to escape. If you hang out until you're trained, you'll be sweet."

"No. I won't."

He rubbed his hands together. "Okay, let's get on with it."

I sighed. There was no use trying to change his mind.

We started my blocking training like nothing had been said and I had to endure another kind of torture with Xander digging up painful memories again.

By the time we'd finished training and had dinner, I was feeling like an emotional wreck. Having Xander dig up the most personal stuff and even old arguments I'd had with Adamo and Jace years ago, together with everything else, was taking its toll.

I'd told Daniel over dinner that there were no cameras in the bathrooms, so Daniel took my hand once we'd entered my room and led me into the bathroom. He wrapped his arms around me as I took a deep breath and let it out slowly and held him close.

"Has Sarinda mentioned doing any blocking training with you?"

"No. I'm reluctant to ask in case she says yes, because I don't want her poking around in my head too."

"I wish I didn't have to do it. It's really getting to me, and not just because he can see it all. It's stuff that happened a long time ago and I don't want to relive it."

"That must suck. So how long do you have to do it for?"

"Until I can block him out. Stopping him getting in is easy, but once he's in there, he goes for the most painful or personal memories and I can't think straight. I don't know how to do it. Nothing I've tried works."

He rubbed my back and started making circular motions, which felt so good that I was able to relax a little more. The knowledge that we weren't being watched helped too.

I rested my cheek against his and enjoyed the buzzing sensations. It helped knowing I didn't have to endure this alone. I couldn't get out of here yet, but I could lose myself in Daniel and forget for a while.

He pressed little kisses on my neck and I sucked in a breath. I closed my eyes and savoured the way it made me feel.

His kisses ran all the way up to my mouth and I kissed him back with enthusiasm. The temperature seemed to rise in the room and I couldn't get enough of him. I pulled him closer and was lost in his kisses.

It was a while before we stopped to catch our breath.

Daniel gave me a smile that melted my heart, then he turned serious, putting his hands on my upper arms. *"Now. We need to be careful."*

"What do you mean?"

"We don't want to get carried away. We don't want little Lenninas running around."

My chest was tight. *"That's the last thing I want right now. Imagine what it's gonna be like for their baby, growing up in here."*

He squeezed me tight again. *"Yeah. They'll run tests to see if it has the abilities that they're hoping for, but the DNA will only show if they have the marker and whether they may develop Talent when they grow up."*

"Don't Xander and Sarinda realise that they'll have to live here till the baby's Talent manifests at puberty?"

I held him for a long while, feeling exhausted, then he suggested we get some sleep.

"Good idea."

We took it in turns using the bathroom, then climbed under the covers, even though it was warm enough to not need them.

I wondered if whoever was watching the camera feeds would get bored and stop watching.

———— ★·☆·★ ————

The next day, we were led into a large training room with about a dozen people standing in groups of two. They were all wearing black, one-piece clothing that looked a lot like a ship-suit, but the material was covered in a chequered pattern.

Xander walked up to Sarinda, who was standing at the front of the room. They both wore the black suits. She and Xander exchanged a look, which probably meant they were speaking telepathically, and she stepped aside so he could address the small crowd.

"Okay, everyone. These are our newest recruits, Lennina Callista and Daniel Javolo. They are both Rated T1 for telepathy and kinetics. Please make them feel welcome." Xander paused and smiled while a few of the people nodded or murmured greetings. He turned to us. "Lennina. Daniel. Today you will start combat training. You will learn how to fight and defend yourselves using your Talent and hand-to-hand combat."

CHAPTER 29

I Didn't Ask for This

My mouth dropped open. "Whoah, wait a minute. No one said anything about learning to fight. We're supposed to be learning how to control our Talent so we can go home."

"This *is* part of your training. You need to have full control over your mind and body to achieve full control of your Talent."

Daniel stepped forward. "These are things we can learn back on our home planets. We only need basic stuff right now and we've learnt that already. We need to go home, man. We need to speak to Rowen. Now."

"You don't get to tell me what to do, okay? Just calm the fuck down. You've been told that when we deem you ready, you'll be on the next flight outta here."

I was beginning to doubt that very much. How long was it going to take to learn control?

The most frustrating part was, I was already *in* control. I was sure that neither of us were a danger to anyone. That was just a bunch of Tauren crap to keep us here.

Xander ushered us over toward the rest of the group. There were five women and five men, still standing in pairs. "These are our trainees. All Talented. All with the Lightning. All Connected like you two."

A weird shiver went down my spine.

Xander clapped his hands and rubbed them together. "Alrighty then. Let's get started. We'll start by doing five laps around the training room, then some warm-up exercises. We'll pair off for some sparring and I'll teach the newcomers some basics." He took a deep breath. "Okay, go."

The group started jogging as one and when Daniel and I didn't follow, Xander rolled his eyes. "What are you two waiting for? Get moving."

"This isn't right," I protested.

"Get your arses moving, Lenni, or I'll zap you."

"Don't call me Lenni!"

"Go!"

Daniel and I shared a glance. We didn't have a choice and we knew it. We'd seen what could happen if we didn't comply, so we started jogging.

After we'd done the five laps and the warm-ups, Sarinda ran through everyone's names, which I forgot instantly. I couldn't concentrate on anything. I was still reeling. We weren't getting out of here for a long time.

Sarinda went to work with the other trainees and Xander stayed to get us started on the basics.

He went into some explanations of how to make a fist and punch correctly because I had no clue. I listened and tried to keep up, but the whole time I was thinking I didn't want to be here and didn't want to learn how to fight.

I complained to Daniel through telepathy and he understood. *"But you know, if you'd known this stuff a few weeks back, you could have avoided the black eye and the broken ribs."*

That got my attention. Maybe learning to defend myself against Malvolio would be worth it. I couldn't get away from him in here and he could turn violent again without warning.

I lifted my chin and straightened my shoulders. I would do this.

"That's better," Xander said. "You'll get it in no time."

But I didn't. I got the punches and blocks and kicks okay, but when it came to actually turning to a person and trying to hit them, I couldn't do it properly. I didn't want to hurt Daniel and was worried that if I gave my punches some strength and he failed to block in time, I'd hit him in the face.

Xander rolled his eyes. "Just do it, Lennina. Daniel will block it." He sighed. "Look. I'll do it. I'm an expert and I will block your punches."

He took Daniel's place and I tried, but still couldn't commit to striking hard.

"Just hit me already," Xander growled.

"Getting angry with me won't help," I told him.

He let his hands drop. "You're useless. I'm wasting my time. You think I don't have anything better to do? I could be over with Sarinda training the *real* recruits. The people who want to be here."

"You got that right. We don't want to be here."

He rolled his eyes again. "I told you. You're not going anywhere until you've completed your training. You're getting all this expert training for free and all you do is whinge and whine."

"I didn't ask for this. *Any* of this. I didn't ask to be Talented. I was just doing my job and planning to go home and all this shit happened."

"Well, I've got news for you, Sunshine, none of us asked for this. Talent just hits you upside the head one day and all you can do is learn how to deal with it. Now that you have it, you need to master it, so it don't master you. You'll never get anywhere if you don't, and you'll never get out of here. So shut up and hit me."

"But—"

"Just hit me!"

I swung at him and his arm came up so fast that I barely saw it as he knocked my arm aside with ease.

"Okay, again."

I tried again with the same result.

"Again."

I kept going, putting more into it each time, and managed to not hit him once.

By the time he said stop, I was exhausted. I stood and watched him spar with Daniel for a while and was surprised at how well Daniel could fight.

I flinched every time one of them got in a hit, but forced myself to watch so I could learn. Feeling the blows land on Daniel's body and arms was hard to deal with as well.

When it was my turn again, Xander wanted me to practice blocking. My heart raced as I put my arms up in a defensive position.

Xander advanced and lunged at me with a jab to the stomach. I blocked too slowly and was glad when he pulled the punch just short of hitting me.

"Too slow, Nina. Try again."

"Don't call me Nina!" I snapped. "*No one* calls me that."

Except my brother, Adamo.

"Alright, settle down. Just trying to be friendly — and that one's pretty."

"Well, stop with the nicknames."

He rolled his eyes and took up the correct fighting stance. "Okay. Again."

I got ready and he went for my face this time. I was too slow again and his fist connected with my jaw, sending me backward to the mat.

The night Malvolio hit me flashed through my mind and Daniel rushed forward. "Lennina! Are you okay?"

CHAPTER 30
That's Just Twisted

I just lay on my back with my jaw on fire, making no attempt to get up. "No. Not really."

Xander stepped forward. "Leave her be, Javolo. She has to learn to shake it off and keep fighting."

Daniel stepped in front of him. "Why did you hit her? She's clearly not ready to block real hits yet."

"It's the only way she's gonna learn, man. Once she feels what a real punch feels like, she's more likely to block faster to avoid being hit again."

"She already knows thanks to that arsehole Malvolio!"

"What are you talking about?"

"Malvolio gave her a black eye and three broken ribs a couple of weeks ago. Didn't they tell you anything?"

"They didn't tell me that." He frowned. "You're full of Tauren shit. Broken ribs take longer than a couple weeks to heal."

"Yeah, but she was healed by one of the aliens from Kronos."

"What?"

I sat up and my head spun. "I tried to tell you the other day. The Ghosts are real. They are called Ampari. They're telepathic and telekinetic like us and they have the power to heal."

His eyes widened. "And one healed you?"

"Yes. He healed Daniel too. Surely you know that Daniel was injured in the tunnel collapse? They really didn't tell you anything, did they?"

"I guess not."

I somehow managed to drag myself up off the floor while Xander made sure Daniel didn't help me.

"Let's go again," Xander said.

Despite what he'd said, he took it easier on me for the rest of the training session. He only managed to punch me in the stomach and the upper arm before we were done.

──── ★·☆·· ────

By the end of the day, I was battered and bruised, and I could punch, kick, and block with some degree of competence, but I knew I had a long way to go before I could use what I'd learnt to defend myself properly.

The more I thought about Malvolio and the fact that I was trapped in here with him — especially when he was able to walk in whenever he felt like it — the more I wanted to learn to fight.

While we were training, I'd avoided sparring with Daniel as much as I could. I didn't want to hurt him, which was kind of stupid because I probably wouldn't have landed a punch anyway. But I couldn't handle thinking of him getting hurt again. Each time Xander had gotten through his defences, I cringed and withdrew a little from the fighting area. It wasn't just because I could feel the pain. Thoughts of him trapped underground and the horrific pain we'd been in haunted me.

I knew it was silly. Maybe I should have spoken to the counsellor about this fear of Daniel getting hurt, but I couldn't take him seriously. It was like they'd dragged some random person in and told him to pretend to be my shrink, and he'd copied what he'd seen of psychologists in HoloMovies. The lines were so cliché. Surely a real psychologist wouldn't say that rubbish.

We walked back to the cafeteria afterward training and I kept to myself. I noticed Daniel glancing my way, but I didn't want to talk.

We ate in silence and I was glad he gave me some space to think.

Once we'd finished eating, Daniel turned to me. *"You okay?"*

I sighed. *"Yeah. Just trying to take it all in, you know?"*

He smiled. *"Yeah. It's all a bit much, even for me, and I know some of it already. I can give you some help if you need it. If you have any questions."*

I smiled. *"Thanks."*

I looked over at Sarinda and Xander eating quietly and probably having a telepathic conversation too. I was still shocked that she was bringing a baby into the world.

Then it hit me. My chest felt heavy.

Katoa wanted this to happen. They wanted us to *breed*.

"Lennina? What is it?"

I looked into his eyes. *"I think I know why we're suddenly allowed to see each other and share a bathroom. They want us to have babies. They want us to create more Talents that might have the Lightning ability."*

His eyebrows rose. *"You think so?"*

"Yes. Think about it. Xander telling me there are no cameras in the bathrooms, then hinting at what he and Sarinda get up to in there, then telling me she's pregnant."

Daniel looked like he'd eaten something sour. *"I think you're right. That's just twisted."*

We headed back to our rooms with our watchdogs in tow and I thought of the Ampari. *"We haven't seen or heard from Allador,"* I said. *"I hope he's alright."*

He took my hand. *"Me too. He risked a lot coming up here."*

"I wonder if he's in trouble with the other Ampari. Maybe they didn't want him to show himself to you. Maybe healing us was forbidden or something."

"Could be. I wish we knew what was happening with him. We really need to try to speak to him. To the other Ampari too."

"Yeah, but how?"

He frowned. *"I'm not sure. Allador has come up here a few times already. Maybe we can get him here again."*

I thought about it. *"Sometimes I would just think about him and he appeared. We could try that."*

"Yeah. It's worth a try."

I stopped in the middle of the hallway and closed my eyes, thinking of Allador. I pictured him in my mind. I even called out to him a couple of times. Nothing. Not even a feeling of connecting to him in my mind. I couldn't help feeling disappointed.

"No. Nothing. I can't feel or hear anything."

Daniel sighed. *"Neither can I, but it was worth trying."* He ran a hand through his hair. *"We'll have to go down there and see if we can speak to them that way."*

I looked up at his face as we started walking again. *"How are we going to do that?"*

"Stow away on one of the shuttles once we get out of here. We know there's air down there, but we will still need to grab some oxygen masks. The ones used by the shuttle crew while they're offloading the Diggers in their Mech-suits and receiving the Amakio will be perfect. I know where they keep them."

"Sounds like we need a plan. Another one."

CHAPTER 31

Not Bad for a First Attempt

Three days into our combat training, I was feeling totally exhausted and wasn't getting any better at it. I was still determined to learn, but had to face the fact that I wasn't a fighter.

So that meant I'd have to try harder to get it right.

Xander had pushed me harder and the hits I'd taken when I'd failed to block his punches and kicks had hurt more than I'd let on. I was feeling like a walking bruise.

Daniel had some bruises as well, but nowhere near the amount that I did.

I could tell my injuries bothered him, especially when he wasn't allowed to help me afterward.

I was grateful that our Talent — or the Lightning — had changed our bodies so that as each day passed, the blows hurt less and we actually healed faster. I wished it had've kicked in sooner.

We needed to somehow learn to block out each other's pain, that was becoming clear. It was difficult to concentrate on defending myself against Xander while Daniel received a punch to the gut from Sarinda.

After our morning warm-up, Xander clapped his hands together. "To-day, we're gonna be teaching you how to use your Lightning abilities."

Before I could ask what he meant, Sarinda entered the room. "Okay, I will partner with Daniel and Xander will partner with Lennina. We'll get you started before you can spar."

Did they mean that we'd get to use Lightning to attack people like Xander did to me?

I turned to Xander. "Do you mean—"

"Yes. You're gonna be able to zap things. Let's get started."

We sat on the mats, facing each other.

"In case you're wondering, all the door locks are heavily insulated, so you can't zap your way out of here."

Damn.

I hadn't thought of it, but I would have eventually.

"Okay. It's hard to explain, but easy to do once you know what you're looking for. You have to feel for the Lightning deep inside yourself. It's in there, waiting to be unleashed. You've already let it loose on Malvolio, so it will probably be easier for you to find than for Danny Boy. Once you've found it, you need to be able to direct it out of your body and into one of the targets over there on the wall."

A panel slid away to reveal a row of targets on the wall that were covered in scorch marks. I shivered. Could I do that?

I'd already done it once, so logic said I could.

"The targets have sensors built into them that measure the strength of the blast, so we can help you learn to control the amount of power released. Too much and you could kill someone."

He paused and let that sink in.

I suppressed a shiver. I couldn't imagine killing a person.

"Close your eyes and concentrate. Remember how it felt just before you struck out at Malvolio. It would have felt hot."

I did as he said but reliving that incident wasn't pleasant. I remembered the heat that built up inside me and after a number of attempts, could feel it in my gut. Xander was right. It did feel like it was sitting waiting to be released.

"Okay, now what do I do with it?"

"Stand up. Push it outward and into your hand. Your right hand if you're right-handed. Otherwise use your left. Once it's travelled down your arm and into your hand, give it a great big shove toward the first target on the wall."

I stood. I reached out my right hand and felt the Lightning gather in my arm and pushed it down to my hand. I looked at the target and pushed hard. A spark shot out across the room and blasted the wall to the right of the target.

Xander whistled. "Not bad for a first attempt. Maybe you'll do better at this than hand-to-hand."

I hoped so, because I couldn't see my hand-to-hand getting better any time soon.

I jumped at the sound of a Lightning blast on the other side of the room and turned to see that Daniel had blasted one of the other targets.

Xander smirked. "Looks like Digger Boy has worked it out too. We'll have you trained in no time."

I couldn't help smiling. The sooner we got out of here, the happier I'd be.

He turned to me. "Okay, let's do it again. You need to learn control. I want you to be able to hit the middle of the target every time. We'll work on the strength once you hit the target and it can measure the force of it."

It was easier to find the Lightning this time, but not so easy to hit the middle of the target.

"What do I have to do to get it on target? Do I aim with my arm or my hand?"

"Neither. You have to picture where you want it to go in your mind, and it will go there. Your arm is just a way to concentrate it into one place so you can release it."

This time, it hit the target's bullseye.

"Now you're getting it, Lenni."

"Don't call me Lenni!"

Chapter 32

We're Gonna Get Out of Here

I wanted to zap him in the face with a bolt of Lightning.

"What am I supposed to call you then?"

"Lennina. Or even Callista."

"You're no fun."

"I'm not here to have fun — especially not with you. I'm here to learn."

We practiced until almost lunch time and I worked on my accuracy and strength. Xander explained the strengths needed to shock, incapacitate, or kill. I paid attention and practiced carefully. I wanted full control over this ability.

Xander looked over to where Daniel was practicing with Sarinda. "Okay. Let's try some sparring."

Adrenalin shot through me. I remembered what it felt like to be on the receiving end of one of Xander's zaps. "How do I block the Lightning?"

He smirked. "I'll show you."

We walked over to the others and Xander asked Sarinda how Daniel was doing.

She smiled. "He's a natural."

I couldn't help smiling at Daniel. He looked pretty chuffed.

Xander rubbed his hands together. "Let's go through blocking techniques, then get down to business."

Sarinda nodded.

She explained how to build up a shield in front of your body with the Lightning. It wasn't visible to the naked eye, but you could feel it.

Once we were able to create one, we practiced for about half an hour until we could put up a shield within two seconds, which was still too slow, but we were assured that we would be able to get it right with more practice.

Sarinda clicked her fingers. "Let's go eat. I'm starving."

I was thankful that Xander and Sarinda didn't sit with us while we ate, but they weren't far away.

Daniel put a hand on mine as it rested on the table. *"Isn't it nice of them to teach us the skills we need to get out of this hell hole?"*

I couldn't help the grin that spread across my face. *"That's exactly what they're doing."*

He bit into his piece of toast. *"We just need to hang out long enough to master the Lightning. We can do this."*

I hoped Malvolio stayed away now that I'd blasted him across the room.

"If Malvolio comes near you, you can tell him to back off or you'll zap his arse."

I chuckled. It wasn't really that funny, but the way Daniel said it, I couldn't help myself.

"Cal?" My eyes snapped to his. *"We're gonna get out of here and we're gonna help the Ampari."*

I smiled. *"Yes. And tell everyone there's air down there. I don't care if they make us sign a gag order. I'll sign it if it shuts them up, then as soon as we're away from here, I'll tell the universe."*

He smiled. *"Sounds like a plan."*

Back in the training room, my nerves were on edge again. What if I wasn't quick enough to block the shots?

Daniel squeezed my hand. *"You got this."*

I wished I shared his confidence.

Sarinda stepped forward.

"You will be issued special clothing like ours." She waved a hand at herself and Xander. "They are made from a fire-retardant material and they actively dampen electrical currents."

That would be handy.

Xander rubbed his hands together, which was starting to grate on me, and said, "Let's get rolling. Lennina is with me and Daniel with Sarinda."

"Not this time," Sarinda said. "I want to see how Lennina is progressing."

Xander looked pissed, but he didn't say anything.

Sarinda took me to the other side of the training room where she'd been training Daniel and I tried to prepare myself.

Sarinda looked at me like she was sizing me up. "So, you were Malvolio's girl, huh?"

What? Why do you want to know that? "I was. Not anymore. I wish I'd never met him."

"What happened? Why would you hook up with Daniel and pass up that money bag?"

"He broke my ribs. And I wasn't in it for the money anyway."

"I would have been, but I guess broken ribs is a deal-breaker."

"You got that right."

She cleared her throat. "Alright, let's get moving. You need to know that hitting another Talent with the Lightning Touch doesn't hurt them as much as it does when you hit a Normie."

"A Normie?"

"Yeah. A normal being. That also includes Talents without the Lightning Touch. It affects them the same."

"Okay. I'll have to remember that."

"Yes, because you can kill them."

"Yeah. Xander told me."

"You can get yourself into some trouble if you go around killing people. Why do you think you're here learning control?"

I cringed.

Some *trouble?* It would be more than just 'some' trouble.

Maybe they *were* just making sure we were properly trained. But that didn't excuse torturing me. That wasn't legal anywhere within the Federated Planets.

"Now, I'll get you to try to hit me first and I'll block you."

She took up a fighting stance, so I copied her.

"Okay. Go."

I shot a bolt of Lightning her way, but it hit her shield and dissipated into the air in front of her. It actually looked quite pretty as it scattered in all directions.

"It's beautiful, I know, but you can't be standing there admiring it like a moron while your opponent is firing the next shot. So pay attention to me at all times. Got it?"

I nodded. "Got it."

As I blasted her shield again, I felt a large jolt of Lightning to my chest, making me cry out. How had she blasted me without me seeing it?

My brain put the information into perspective and I knew what had happened. I turned to see Daniel lying on the floor and rushed over to him, an image of him in the Infirmary with tubes and wires everywhere filling my mind and my breaths coming out in shallow bursts.

Chapter 33

I Feel a Connection to You

Xander stepped in my way. "Whoah, there, Sunshine." I anticipated his move and ducked around him, my heart pounding in my ears. "Leave him be."

"Daniel! Are you okay?"

His clothing was scorched where he'd been hit.

He groaned and tried to smile. "I'll live."

My heart pounded in my ears. Why did I feel like this?

Xander wasn't happy. "Don't you help him."

"Shut up, Xander."

He crossed his arms. "Don't talk to me like that, or I'll zap your arse, too."

At that point, I didn't care if he did.

I was light-headed. After Daniel had come so close to death in the tunnels...

I couldn't do this. I couldn't be here. "I gotta go." I stood and strode toward the door, heart hammering in my chest.

"Come back here, Lennina."

I ignored Xander and he didn't follow. Raynar immediately left his post near the door when he realised that I was leaving the room and I broke into a run. He managed to keep up with me all the way back to my room.

I went straight to the bathroom and splashed some water on my face. The person staring back at me in the mirror was someone I hardly recognised. I looked thinner and my eyes were kind of haunted.

I was no longer the carefree Nav Operator with a positive attitude and a love for life and music. I hadn't been able to play any music and it hurt my soul to think of it. I hadn't even heard any music since I'd been locked up in here. Maybe I could request a small music player of some kind to keep in here. It might help keep my sanity.

I wondered if Daniel was having the same problem. He shared my love of music. Maybe he was missing his drum kit.

I dried my face and curled up on my side on the bed. I closed my eyes and practiced my relaxation techniques and realised Daniel was calling me.

"Lennina? Are you okay?"

"Sorry. I had to go. I can't... I saw you lying there and..."

"It's okay, Cal. I'm okay. There's no permanent damage."

"I don't know why I'm like this. I can't do this. We have to get out now."

"Breathe. Calm down. Don't do anything you'll regret. It's gonna be okay. We'll get through this. We need this to help us get out. If we don't learn, Xander and Sarinda will kick our arses and we won't make it ten metres."

I sighed. He was right. And I hadn't even realised I wasn't breathing.

"Are you sure you're okay?"

"I guess... I will be. I just need some time alone."

"Okay. I'll see you when I've finished here."

I didn't answer. I didn't want to think of them continuing to fight. I couldn't deal with it. How was I going to get through this? I wished I could call Mum and Adamo and tell them everything. They'd taken us beyond the normal training that they'd give to a Talent; this was military stuff. I needed to be able to tell someone what was actually going on here and I really needed to just go home.

Before training the next day, we'd been given our black suits. They fit perfectly and were extremely comfortable and flexible. I wondered what sort of technology went into developing something like this for us to wear.

Once we were warmed up, we started our training by practicing our

Lightning abilities before moving on to hand-to-hand combat. It was only Xander and I this time.

He started by lecturing me about walking out on a lesson and I scowled at him.

Later, when we were going through how to throw someone over your shoulder, it seemed like he was holding on to me for just a moment longer than he should and it irked me.

Was it my imagination? Was I reading too much into it? I wasn't sure, but I was uncomfortable with it.

I hadn't talked to Daniel much. We were busy anyway. Or was that my excuse for not wanting to speak to him? I didn't know why I felt that way, but I needed to be in my own head for a bit. I'd been asleep when he'd finished training the night before and I hadn't heard him come into my room. I hadn't woken up when he snuggled up next to me.

In the afternoon, Xander and I headed to our original training room to work on my telekinesis.

We sat in the chairs and I tried to get comfortable. Xander clapped his hands and rubbed them together. "So, you're from Azaeli, huh? Whereabouts?"

I tried not to react to the hand rubbing; it really bugged me. "Turrisi. That's in the Eastern Quarter of Aalaya."

His eyebrows drew together. "Oh. Okay. Never heard of it."

"It's pretty small. Where are you from?"

"Azaeli."

That surprised me. "Whereabouts?"

"Campisi. Do you know where that is?"

I resisted the urge to roll my eyes. "Yeah. Everyone knows where Campisi is."

He leaned closer. "So, we're from the same planet. Same culture. No wonder we have so much in common."

What? "No, we don't."

"Yeah. The same drive and determination. We're compatible. We know each other pretty well. I've seen your memories and I know who you really are. More than Digger Boy. More than anyone alive. That's something special."

"You only saw my memories because you keep invading my mind. That's not anything special. It's downright creepy."

His eyebrows rose. "You think I'm creepy?"

I crossed my arms. "Yes. I don't enjoy having you in my head."

"It's all part of your training. Nothin' personal. I'm only doing my job. You understand, don't ya?"

I frowned. "Yeah. But I don't have to like it."

"No. Fair enough." He leaned even closer. "So you forgive me?"

"I guess..."

"Good, because I feel a connection to you."

"What?" Where was this coming from?

Before I knew what was happening, he closed the gap between us, pulled me into an embrace and pressed his lips to mine. The jolt of electricity made me gasp.

CHAPTER 34
Come Back, Darlin'

My brain took a moment to catch up as he tried to deepen the kiss and I pulled away from him. "What are you doing?"

His arms were still locked around me, so I only managed to get a few centimetres away from his face.

"We were meant to be together, you and me. Can't you feel how strong the Lightning Connection is between us? Forget the others."

"No! Let me go!"

"But, Honey. We could be so good together."

I pushed against his chest and only managed to move back a little with my arms still crossed. "Let go of me, Xander!"

I managed to free my right arm.

"No. I never wanna let you go. We could—"

My fist crashing into his jaw cut off his words and his arms dropped, giving me the opportunity to get away from him.

"Oww! That hurt!" Then, "Hey, you've got a good right hook when you put your heart into it." He realised I'd made it to the door already. "Come back, darlin'. I'm sorry! I'll keep my hands to myself. I promise."

I didn't hear any more after that. I was too far away.

My eyes stung with unshed tears. Why did he do that? What made him think I felt that way about him? What about Sarinda? Didn't he care about her? What about their baby? What about Daniel? What would I tell him?

I let the anger rush through me. How dare he? I hadn't done anything to indicate that I liked him that way.

Had I?

A globe popped somewhere above me, but I didn't care.

I should have known. I should have seen it coming. I should have stopped it before it got to that point.

Maybe I wanted him to kiss me. Was it something subconscious? I searched, but couldn't find anything in me that would want to be with Xander. Nothing at all. I was repulsed by him. So what was it? Why didn't I do something? I was pathetic.

I wandered through the halls, wishing Raynar wasn't trailing behind me, wishing I could escape. I wished I could go to the Observation Deck out in the main section of the station and stare out into space. Seeing Kronos below so close through the windows was always calming.

But I had no such outlet. I had no idea why I'd thought of the Observation Deck. Maybe because of how trapped I felt.

I ended up in the training facility and started jogging around the track. As I jogged, Daniel came up beside me out of nowhere. "Hey, you."

"Hey."

Daniel was the last person I wanted to be around right now. I felt so guilty and confused.

Well, maybe not the last. Xander would be the last.

He frowned. "Are you okay?"

I slowed down and then stopped. "Yeah. I'm fine." I tried to smile as we caught our breath.

"Then why the tears?" Those green eyes didn't miss a thing.

I hadn't realised I was crying. I opened my mouth, unsure of what I was going to say, when Xander walked up behind Daniel and put an arm around his shoulders. "Hey, there, Danny Boy. How's it goin'?"

My whole body tensed. What was he up to?

Daniel shrugged him off. "Fine."

"Lenni here is a great kisser, isn't she?" He actually winked at me as he spoke.

Adrenalin spiked through me; I couldn't believe he'd just come out and said it.

Daniel looked at me. "What?"

The smirk on Xander's face made me want to punch him again. "Go on, darlin'. Tell him how much you enjoyed our kiss."

I clenched my fists. "You piece of Tauren shit!"

The way Xander stumbled backward made me realise I'd actually pushed him with my mind. I stepped forward to let him know I'd do it again if he didn't go right now.

He raised both hands in surrender, but the smirk was back as he turned away. Was this payback for rejecting him?

I turned back to Daniel and my face burned. What could I say?

"I'm sorry."

The hurt in his eyes was tearing me apart. "What happened? Did you two really kiss?"

"I..." I couldn't talk. Fresh tears stung my eyes.

"Why didn't you tell me?"

"It only just happened before I came in here. And it didn't mean anything."

His eyebrows rose. "Didn't mean anything?"

I clenched my jaw. "No. I don't like him that way."

"But you still kissed him?"

"*No!* He kissed me. I just felt guilty for not stopping him."

"You didn't stop him?"

"No. I mean, I *did* stop him. I punched him in the mouth." My hands were shaking.

He frowned. "I'm confused. Why did you say you didn't stop him if you punched him?"

"I mean I didn't stop the conversation. I didn't see where it was headed. I should have known."

He stepped forward. "How could you have known he was going to do that?"

I clenched my fists. "I don't know. I just... I should have seen the signs and shut him down before he even thought about it."

"I don't see how you could've done that. You're not a mind reader... Well, okay, you are, but you know what I mean."

"Yeah. I do."

"So don't be so hard on yourself."

"But I feel so bad."

"Don't. He's a jerk. He'll get his."

Daniel turned on his heel and strode away.

Oh, no.

He was going to find Xander.

"Wait! Don't get yourself in trouble over this!"

CHAPTER 35

This Was What I Needed

He kept walking. *"I'll be fine."*

I followed him and he found Xander in the corridor near the cafeteria.

He didn't even say anything, just walked up and punched Xander in the face, knocking him to the floor.

I waited for the retaliation. Waited for someone to stun him or for Xander to zap him. But there was nothing.

Daniel walked away while Xander sat up rubbing his chin, and he was actually smirking at me.

I turned and followed Daniel on shaky legs.

★·☆··

Later that night when we were in my room, I was restless. Anxious. I wanted to be alone.

Why do I feel like this?

Daniel sensed it and tried to hold onto my hands. I turned away and pulled my hands from his, then immediately wished I hadn't.

"Why are you pulling away? Have I done something wrong?"

"No."

"Is it him? Do you have feelings for Xander?"

My eyes snapped to his. "*No!* He's a jerk."

"Then what is it?"

I ran a hand through my hair. "I don't know!" *"I just feel like I need to be alone. I need to get away."*

He took a tiny step forward. *"Maybe it's not me you're trying to get away from. Maybe it's this place."*

"Yeah. No. Maybe. I don't know."

I moved back again toward the bathroom.

Daniel moved toward me, thought better of it, and leaned against the wall. *"Why are you still avoiding me?"*

"I don't know."

He clenched his fists. *"It's killing me inside, Lennina. I love you so much. I thought you felt the same, but now I'm not so sure."*

"I do."

He ran a hand through his hair. *"What's wrong, then?"*

The frustration built up inside me. I felt like I was going to explode. *"I don't know. I keep seeing you trapped underground in my head and I can't shake it. I can't handle it."*

"Have you told the counsellor?"

I sighed. *"No. He is an idiot."*

"But it might help—"

"It won't!" *"Nothing will."*

"There must be something you can do to work it out—"

"I don't want to lose you, okay?" Tears ran down my cheeks. *"The devastation I felt when I thought you were dead, I don't ever want to feel like that again. Every time you get hurt, I feel this ache in my chest."*

Tears welled in his eyes. *"I feel it when you get hurt. When they tortured you, I felt it too — the first part anyway — but there was also the knowledge that you were being hurt and I couldn't do anything about it. Unfortunately, it's something we can't avoid. There's no way to avoid pain in our lives — especially in here — so we have to learn to deal with it. And we can deal with it together. I'm here for you. Always."*

I looked into his eyes. He was right. Avoiding him wasn't the answer. I fell into his open arms and let the tears flow freely. This was what I needed.

"I'm sorry," I whispered.

It wouldn't fix the problem, but it was easier to share the burden.

He guided me to the bed and we sat down together. *"We'll get this training right and we'll look out for each other. We'll make sure that we make it out of here in one piece. I promise I'll do everything I can to keep us safe."*

I buried my face in the crook of his neck and held him tighter. *"Thank you."*

He squeezed me tighter. *"Let's get under the blankets."*

I nodded. We'd already given our watchers too much of a show. We crept under the covers and put them over our heads. Being in his arms gave me comfort. I needed his strong arms to make me feel like he could maybe keep his promise and keep us safe. I had to hold on to the hope that we'd survive this hell hole and finally get out of here.

His kisses were tentative at first, but soon I felt like I was on fire as our hands roamed freely. Everything faded away and was forgotten. I needed to forget for a while. And I wished we could do more than just kiss.

—— ⋆·☆·⋆ ——

It had been two weeks since Xander kissed me and I still wanted to punch him in the face again.

Daniel and I had been working on how to block out each other's pain by practicing it during our free time, then moved on to doing it during training. It wasn't something that came naturally to us, but if we concentrated, we could do it.

It was another thing we needed to do before we could get out of here, because it was something they could use against us.

Xander turned up at my door one morning telling me we were about to try something new. I scowled.

"Come on. It's been two weeks. Get over it."

I'd hardly spoken to him and wasn't about to start now.

Every day had been the same. Wake up too early, eat, train, eat, train, eat, spend some time with Daniel — which usually involved practicing pain blocking — then sleep. No weekends. No time off. No Vid calls to home. No way to get the message out about what was happening to us.

I followed Xander to a room I hadn't been in before. It was set up much the same as the small training room we'd been using — minus the table — with some extra seats on the edge of the room.

I cringed when I saw Malvolio sitting in one of them. I wondered how long he'd been in the Infirmary and wished he was still there. Then he wouldn't be here.

Dr Rowen sat next to him with her fake smile in place, but Malvolio looked pissed.

Rowen stood and approached us. "Good morning, trainees. Today, you will work together to try to increase your power."

Daniel frowned. "How do we do that?"

"Xander will show you how."

Great.

She looked at Xander expectantly and he stepped forward. "I'll give you a demonstration. Lennina, if you'll sit in that chair, I'll sit in the other and we'll get started."

At least he didn't rub his hands together this time.

I sat facing him and he took my hands in his. I tried to pull them away, but he held tight.

"Is this really necessary?" I asked. The last thing I wanted was him touching me.

"I'm afraid it is. To be able to combine power, you need to be touching."

But I didn't want to combine my power with his.

Daniel stepped forward and opened his mouth, but Rowen shook her head. "Do you want to learn how to do this?"

Daniel gave a small nod, but it was clear that he wasn't happy.

"Then stay put and watch closely."

"Okay, close your eyes," Xander said. "We need to both find the Lightning inside and bring it forth, push it out, and combine it in the space between us."

"Can't I just do this with Daniel? We both know how to bring out the Lightning."

He held my hands a little tighter. "Just do it, Lennina."

I sighed and closed my eyes. It was easy to find the Lightning and push it out like he'd said, but when it came to combining it with Xander's, it wouldn't join with his. I tried to get it to mix, but it stayed separate and was hard to keep contained.

"Why isn't it working?"

I gave it another push and before I knew what had happened, I felt myself being thrown backward and my eyes shot open as I hit the floor.

CHAPTER 36
You're Both Pathetic

"Lennina! Are you okay?" Daniel was standing over me with his hands out, like he wanted to help me, but knew they wouldn't let him.

I nodded.

The power must have pushed both of us backward as Xander was picking himself up off the floor on the other side of the room.

Rowen stepped forward. "What happened? What went wrong?"

Xander shook his head. "It should have worked."

I stood up and tried to ignore the pain at the back of my head. "I'll tell you what went wrong. It wasn't Daniel. My Lightning power is not meant to combine with yours. You're paired with Sarinda, so stop trying to pair with me!"

I tried to get out of the room, but Raynar stepped in front of the door.

"You're not going anywhere, Callista," Rowen said. "You're going to try again."

I growled in frustration as I ran my fingers across the back of my head and found a huge lump there.

"Lennina, that's—"

"Don't tell me it's not ladylike, Malvolio, or I'll blast you into the next room!"

Rowen stepped in front of me, which was a stupid thing to do right about now. "Now let's calm down, shall we? We're trying to teach you something important, so you need to try again."

"Not with Xander," I snapped.

"You can try it with Daniel." She turned to Xander. "Why did you initiate this with Lennina? That's not how it's been done in the past."

"He's trying to pair with me," I told her.

"I'm not—"

"Yes you are! Don't deny it. I want you to stop it. I don't love you. I don't even like you. I don't want you to touch me again. You saw what happened when you tried to combine your power with mine. We were nearly blown against the walls."

He hung his head. He knew I was right.

We were told to try again, so we stood the chairs back up and this time, when Daniel and I joined hands and closed our eyes, I felt a hand on my arm.

My eyes flew open. *What now?*

Malvolio was pulling my arm, trying to separate us.

I tried to pull my arm out of his grip. "What are you doing? Let me go!"

"I cannot allow this. You're my girl. Don't touch him. I can't stand the thought of you touching him. Being with him."

Daniel stood. "Leave her alone!"

I managed to free my arm, and before I could say anything, Rowen was in Malvolio's face. "Mr Dermid. What do you think you're doing? You know how important this research is. They must be allowed to continue with this exercise."

He looked at her like she'd grown a second head, then seemed to come to his senses. "But she was mine! It was supposed to be me that got the power over Lightning, not this Neanderthal!"

"What do you mean?" I asked.

Did they know about this all along? Was he only with me because of the Lightning?

He looked at me. "It was supposed to be me. How could you fall for this low-breed and give him the power?"

"So you were only with me because you wanted to have the Lightning power?"

"No! I loved you. I still do. We can still make it work, just you and me. Forget about him."

Daniel stepped closer, fists clenched, sparks dancing around them, and Rowen cleared her throat. "Mr Dermid, we've been over this. You do *not* have the DNA markers needed for this to work. And once a bond is formed, you cannot break it. No one else can pair with a bonded individual. We've tested this."

I scowled at them all. "So you knew about this and didn't think it would be a good idea to tell us about it?"

"There was no need." Rowen said. "Not everyone with the markers in their DNA develops Talent, and not all of them develop the Lightning power as well."

"DNA? You tested our DNA and knew we had the markers?"

"Of course. It's company policy to thoroughly test the blood and DNA of all employees—"

"For toxins, but not to see if they might develop psychic abilities! Geez!"

"It's in your contract. We reserve the right to test for any and all abnormalities or anomalies."

She was probably right. "It's still wrong not to tell us." I turned to Malvolio and Xander. "You only wanted power. You're both pathetic."

Xander looked ashamed and Malvolio looked like he was going to punch me.

"Don't even think about touching me ever again, Malvolio. I know how to do more than break your ribs."

CHAPTER 37
Look What I Found

I couldn't believe I'd just threatened him. Again. What had happened to me? They wanted to turn me into a soldier, and I was becoming someone I never wanted to be.

I needed to get out of here and away from them all.

Rowan sighed. "Have you all calmed down? Can we get on with things now?" When no one answered, she told us to sit back down and try again. "Mr Dermid. If you can't control yourself, may I suggest that you leave the room?"

He glared at her.

It was hard to concentrate at first, but we were finally able to do it right. The power was able to combine and I opened my eyes to see a bluish ball about the size of a volleyball hovering in the air, with little sparks of Lightning within it.

"Now what?" I looked around the room and their mouths were hanging open. "What?"

Xander finally answered. "No one's been able to create a ball of power that big before."

"Oh." What could I say? "How big is it supposed to be?"

"Well, there's no set size, I guess, but it's twice the size of even mine and Sarinda's."

Did this mean he would try to pair with me again? I hoped not. Maybe he'd gotten it through his thick head after hitting the floor.

I kept an eye on the ball of power to keep it in place. "What do we do with it now?"

Xander waved a hand dismissively. "Let it dissipate. Letting it go is a good skill to learn."

"How?"

"You'll figure it out."

I rolled my eyes. Some great teacher he turned out to be.

Daniel looked me in the eye. *"Relax, Lennina, and it should recede."*

I smiled at Daniel and did as he said. The ball slowly shrunk and fragmented, and finally vanished. I was exhausted afterward.

Later that day, after combat training and some dinner, Daniel was acting weird. As soon as we entered my room, he pulled me into the bathroom.

"Look what I found."

I gasped. Sitting in his open hand was a destabiliser. *"Where did you get that?"*

He smirked. "I stole it from a guard using telekinesis."

"What are you going to do with it?"

"I thought we could use it to try to build an immunity for when we escape. You know they're gonna hit us with them first chance they get. Maybe we can get it so that it doesn't affect us anymore."

My heart hammered in my chest. *"Are you nuts? You want to use that thing on us?"*

"Yes. It will be horrible, but if it works, we won't be immobilised and they won't be able to stop us from escaping."

"I know, but..." I knew he was right, but the thought of using it on ourselves made me nauseous.

He put a hand on my arm. *"It's okay. I'll go first. Just blast me with it and I'll see how long I can stand it."*

"But you haven't felt the effects before."

He smiled. *"Now's as good a time as any for me to find out."*

I was not comfortable with this. *"Are you sure?"*

"Not really, but you know we have to do this so we can get out of here."

I sighed. *"I know."*

"Just hit me."

"It's really awful."

He squared his shoulders. *"Just do it."*

"Okay."

I pressed the button and immediately felt on edge. I tried to use my Talent, but couldn't. "Umm. There's a flaw in your plan," I told him. "It's affecting both of us."

"Oh, yeah. I forgot."

I lifted my hand and looked at it. I felt like I was shaking all over, but it was steady.

The longer we were exposed, the worse I felt. I couldn't move properly. "Well, this sucks."

The nausea started and built up steadily until I felt like I'd throw up, so I turned the awful thing off and breathed a sigh of relief. Daniel retched and I thought he'd vomit all over my feet.

"That thing is disturbing," he said as he rubbed his arms and legs and face.

"I told you it was bad."

He nodded. *"I think we need to expose ourselves for a shorter period than that — just till the nausea starts — then turn it off, every chance we get."*

I moaned. *"I was afraid you'd say that."*

Knowing it could mean the difference between escape and staying stuck in here didn't make me feel any better about doing it.

Daniel found a spot around behind the drain under the sink to hide the device while I tried to settle my stomach by doing some relaxation techniques. This was gonna take some doing.

The next week involved more of the same. The routine was always the same. The hand-to-hand combat sessions left me bruised and feeling dejected because I wasn't improving that much. The Lightning training made me feel a bit better, but I still needed to work on my shield. I had improved immensely with my telepathy and telekinesis, so I was happy about that.

Blocking training was getting me down. I'd lost count of how many memories had been dragged up and most of them weren't pleasant. If it wasn't for Daniel's love and support, I would have lost my sanity by now.

Daniel was my rock. His arms were a barrier against reality and I could get lost in his kisses at the end of each day. He helped me with some of the difficult moves in combat training and massaged my tired muscles. I'd offer to give him a massage in return, but he'd always refuse.

At least the gruelling sessions with the destabiliser were finally paying off. We could tolerate it for a much longer period without throwing up, but it still made us nauseous.

I had to attend another appointment with the stupid counsellor this morning, but I still felt sick from using the destabiliser for a bit too long the night before. Raynar walked along in silence, but still managed to annoy me.

When I was almost at Lysander's door, I suddenly couldn't bear the thought of talking to him. I stopped walking and closed my eyes.

"Miss Callista? Are you okay?"

I opened my eyes. "No, Raynar. I'm not. And when are you gonna stop calling me Miss Callista?"

"I won't. You're my responsibility. I'm not supposed to get personal with you or be your friend."

"Seriously? You take your job too literally."

He crossed his arms. "You're going to be late for your appointment with Dr Lysander if you don't get moving."

I looked him in the eye. "I'm not going."

CHAPTER 38
What? You Thought She Wouldn't Find Out?

"What?"

"I can't do this today. Reschedule my appointment or whatever. I can't deal with him right now."

"You don't get to choose. You have to go. Plus, if you're feeling like you can't deal with things, it would help to talk about it."

I started walking again and Raynar followed. "Not with him. Have you ever been in to see him? He's an idiot."

"No. He's not for staff. Only the trainees."

"Yeah. You guys probably have a real shrink."

He huffed. "Dr Lysander is a fully qualified psychiatrist."

I turned down a corridor in the opposite direction of Lysander's office. "Doesn't act like it."

"You're going the wrong way."

"I don't care. I'm not going. You can't force me to go."

He made a call to Lysander on his Personal Com and he was told to let me go. I heard Lysander say he didn't want to speak to me if I wasn't going to cooperate.

Yes!

If that's all it took to avoid talking to him, I'd do it every time.

Then I heard, "If it happens again, we'll have to employ strict methods to make her want to come."

My stomach dropped. I didn't want to know what that meant.

I kept walking and pretended I hadn't heard.

There wasn't much I could do, so I ended up back in my room. Not long after the door had swished shut on Raynar's face, it opened again and Malvolio barged in.

I leapt off my bed. "When are you gonna stop barging in here uninvited? Get out!"

"Just hear me out," he pleaded.

I looked at the tiny sparks dancing around my hands.

He followed my line of sight and sucked in a breath. "Lennina. Don't do anything rash. I'm just here to speak to you."

I raised my hands a little to make him more nervous. "What do you want?"

"You weren't at your appointment with Dr Lysander."

I frowned. "So? What's it got to do with you?"

"I have a vested interest in anyone who shows signs of Talent on the station."

"So I've been told, but why? So you can use them to get Lightning powers?"

"No. I'm in charge of this mining operation and the research we are conducting here with the Talents with Lightning powers."

"You'll have to think of something shorter and more catchy to call us."

He frowned. "I'm sorry, what?"

"*Talents with Lightning powers* sounds too long and convoluted, so you'll have to come up with something else, like Lightning Talents, or maybe Sparkies."

The frown deepened. "What are you talking about? I'm trying to have a serious conversation with you, and you're off with the fairies, talking about name changes."

I sighed. "We weren't really having a conversation. You asked me about my appointment. I'm not there because I can't deal with talking to him right now. Plus, he's an idiot."

He lifted his chin. "Lose the attitude, Lennina."

I lifted my hands higher. "Is that a threat?"

He watched the Lightning dance over my fingers. "No. It's good advice for you to follow while you're in here."

I scowled at him. "Just get out. Or I might just give you a shock large enough to give you permanently curly hair."

He took a step back. "You need to report to Xander for another training session."

I groaned. "No. I can't deal with that at the moment."

"You have no choice. You can zap me right now, but you will still be forced to continue your training after your punishment."

A shiver ran down my spine at the thought of having to endure that torture again.

I pointed a finger at him. "I'll go, but not with you tagging along. So I'll tell you again. Get out."

———— ★·☆·· ————

The next day after some combat training, I was supposed to report to Xander for Blocking training again. I needed to hurry up and learn how to block him before I lost my mind.

As I walked slowly through the corridor with my shadow trailing behind me, Sarinda came round a corner and nearly ran into me.

"You bitch! What are you trying to do? First Malvolio, then Daniel, and now you're after Xander too! You're nothing but a whore!"

I wondered how she'd found out and was surprised it had taken three weeks. "I'm not after Xander. I'm not the least bit interested. *He* kissed *me*, not the other way around!"

"He *kissed* you? Fucking hell! I can't believe this is happening! You can't steal someone's partner once they've formed a Connection with someone else."

So she didn't know.

I sighed. "I know that. I'm not trying to steal him. You can have him. But I don't know why you'd want him if he's so willing to cheat on you."

The blast hit me full-force in the chest and I was pushed into the wall behind me. I wasn't expecting it, so I hadn't blocked it at all.

Getting blasted wasn't as painful as it was when we'd started Lightning training and it was getting easier to recover from, but it still sucked.

Once I'd dragged myself into a sitting position, she was gone.

I looked up at a stunned Raynar. "Thanks a lot, Raynar. I thought you were supposed to be my bodyguard."

"No. I'm just here to stop you running away."

"And you've done a brilliant job so far."

"Shut up."

When I arrived at the training room, I didn't want to go in. I clenched my fists. I knew I had to do this again and was not prepared — especially after what had just happened with Sarinda.

The door swished open.

"Xander, tell your girlfriend to leave me alone," I said as a greeting.

"What? What happened?"

I walked in, but didn't sit down.

"Sarinda happened. She's out of control. She blasted me in the chest. She told me to keep away from you, and now she knows you kissed me, you stupid jerk."

He scowled. "How does she know about that?"

"I told her." His eyes widened. "What? You thought she wouldn't find out?"

CHAPTER 39
Get Out and Stay Out!

"Why did you tell her?"

I started pacing. "I thought she already knew, the way she was abusing me. Tell her to back off."

He folded his arms. "Alright, but I doubt she'll listen."

"You better be prepared for whatever she's gonna throw at you. She was pissed."

His face looked pale.

"You're an idiot. You shoulda thought about the consequences before you did it."

He gestured for me to sit. "Let's just get on with our training session."

"Really? Right now?"

"Yes, now. Sit down. Let's start."

I sighed. I knew I couldn't avoid this. I told myself that I needed to learn.

I sat down and got comfortable, but cringed when I let Xander into my mind. I hated this. These memories he kept digging up were too private. I didn't want him to see any of it, and I'd only managed to almost push him out a couple of times. This wasn't working.

He went straight in without even speaking to me and I was dumped into the memory of when Daniel was trapped under the ground down on the planet.

"Suit is telling me... I'm almost... out of air." *He was struggling for coherent thoughts in his mind. I could hear it. I could feel it. They weren't going to make it to him. Surely they were getting close...*

I could feel the panic rising. "Can you hear anything? Any sounds that might mean they're near you?"

There was silence while he listened and it seemed to stretch on forever.
"No," *he finally said.* "Nothin'... Well, at least... I won't die alone..."

"NO! Don't say that!" *I knew it was going to happen, knew I couldn't stop it, but I didn't want him to talk like that.*

He sighed heavily. "Lennina. I need to... to say goodbye... before it's too late... and I can't talk anymore... I feel really weak... I can't breathe properly..."

Oh... no... "No!" *How could I stop him from thinking like that? How could I save him? My heart was breaking... I wanted to scream...*

"I love you..." *he told me.* "I've loved you... for such a long time... and... and... the woman I saw... that night... that I said was... the most beautiful woman... I had... ever... seen... it was you..."

"Oh, Daniel..."

That statement just hit me — went right for the heart. And I melted. And cried harder. I couldn't believe what I'd heard. Surely it wasn't true. I remembered how he'd described her and more tears came flooding down my cheeks.

"She has long dark hair and bright blue eyes that seem to flash at you when she smiles..." It was so... Poetic? Romantic? Yes. It sounded so romantic. Such a beautiful way to describe someone. But he'd used those words to describe me. It warmed my breaking heart.

He'd also said she had "the most perfect bod." I didn't think I had a 'perfect' body, but that was what he'd said from his first impression...

I'd loved his poetic description of my eyes... He'd been talking about me and neither of us knew it... It was too weird...

I smiled through the tears. So that's what he thought when he saw me... That I was beautiful... That was unexpected. I wasn't ugly, I knew that, but I wouldn't have described myself as beautiful. Maybe he was just saying it so I would feel better or something. But that couldn't be right. At the time, he didn't even know it was me...

Then I thought about when I'd met him. I was practically drooling over him. He was gorgeous... and I couldn't stop staring at him... and he kept staring at me...

My thoughts returned to the present. I needed to do something, and fast. But what?

"You're not going to die!" *I told him.* "You can't! Not now! I need you to just... just hang on... they'll be there soon... I just know they will!"

I wondered if he could hear the lie in my voice.

I remembered that Xander was here seeing this. This was wrong. This was something between me and Daniel. I was drawn back into the memory.

There was a pause. My heart was thumping inside my chest, trying to get out through my throat. What was I going to do? Then I realised he hadn't spoken for a while. Was he okay? I started to worry that he had lost consciousness, or worse, and the panic shot through me.

"All along... All this time... It was always you..." *It was like a whisper in my mind. He was barely there. Just a small thread...*

I clung to the thread.

"No... more... air... it says... it's... empty..."

"NO! Oh, crap. Hang in there! Don't die on me! I love you! Daniel! DANIEL!"

I screamed out loud as I pushed Xander out of my mind with all the force I could muster.

"Get out and stay out!" I screamed into his mind.

CHAPTER 40
Xander's Game

I opened my eyes as he almost fell off his chair. His eyes were wide. "H-how did you do that?"

Tears ran down to my chin and I could hardly speak. "I don't know, but we're done here. I blocked you out. End of lesson. You're never going inside my head again!"

Without even thinking, I pushed past his defences and easily made it into his mind. *"How do you like it?"*

He was shocked. I could read his thoughts. He didn't know of anyone who could do what I just did. I wanted to scream. I didn't hesitate. I dove into his memories.

I saw everything from his perspective, which was weird.

I walked over to my father. He was hunched over as if he was in pain. "Father?"

He turned to me with a look of pure hatred on his face. "You."

I took a step back. "What is it?"

"You're one of them," he spat.

I knew what he meant. One of the Talented.

"You're no son of mine! Get out of this house right now!"

I stumbled back away from him. How could he do this? "But, Father! I'm still me. I haven't changed. You can't just kick me out! Where will I go? What will I do?"

"That's no concern of mine. I'll give you an hour to organise your things. Now, get out of my sight!"

I pulled back from the memory, feeling guilty now for invading his privacy. I had to remind myself that he'd been doing the same to me nearly every day for about four weeks.

"Get out of my head!" he said weakly.

It occurred to me that he hadn't stopped me. *"Why didn't you stop me?"*

Xander was breathing heavily. He didn't need to say anything as the truth hit me. He couldn't.

I clenched my fists and dropped the Mind-link. "You can't, can you?" He stared at me with his mouth open. "All this time, you were trying to 'teach' me something that you couldn't even do yourself? Was this all a big joke to you? Just an excuse to dig into my memories and watch me suffer? I can't believe you did this!"

I threw my hands out in front of me, thinking I wanted him far from me, and Lightning flew from my fingers, hitting him in the chest and knocking the chair over backwards.

He yelled out as he landed and let out a string of curses.

I flew out of my chair and ran from the room. I didn't know where I was going, I just knew I had to get away from him.

All the torture he'd put me through, and for what? For something he'd thought was impossible. For his own sick pleasure.

As I walked, I sensed the Lightning running through my veins. I raised a hand. Sparks danced across my fingertips. I needed to release the pent-up energy surging through me. I turned toward the training facility.

Raynar would have been able to see the Lightning dancing over my skin and was smart to keep quiet. One word from him and I might have let him have it.

As I approached the door, it swished open and one of the other trainees walked out, eyes widening. I must have looked pretty wild. I strode in there and found the nearest target. I fired off a dozen or so shots of Lightning straight at the bullseye while everyone in the room stared. Every one of them registered as a kill shot.

Daniel found me in my room pacing the floor.

"What's wrong? I heard you were in the training room blasting the targets."

"I want out of here," I told him. *"Xander's a creep. I can't believe he did this to me."*

His eyebrows rose and he stepped forward. *"What did he do this time?"*

Lightning danced around my hands and up my arms. *"The Blocking training was all a lie! He can't do it and didn't believe it was even possible! He was so surprised when I kicked him out of my head. He'd only used it as an excuse to read my memories. I could kill him! How could he do that?"*

Daniel's fists clenched. *"He's such a fucking bastard! I'll zap him out the nearest airlock!"*

Daniel closed his eyes for a few seconds and took a deep breath. He ignored the sparks and took me into his arms. For a second I wanted to push him away and be by myself, but once I felt the buzzing and the warmth of his arms around me, I knew I needed the comfort only he could give me. I soaked it in and took a slow, deep breath.

I held him tighter. *"We need to hurry up and get out of here. I don't know how much more I can take."*

He squeezed me. *"Hang in there, darlin'. We'll get out of here as soon as we can. Don't you worry."*

"It's not soon enough."

"We can't try until we're ready or we risk their punishment." I cringed. *"I've found out where there's a couple of entries into the service corridors. There's cameras there, of course, but if we're quick, we might be able to get out before they can send someone after us."*

"Or maybe we could blast the cameras."

"Yeah. One door is near the big training room and one's near Lysander's office. I think there's less chance we'll run into people at Lysander's."

"Okay." I took another deep breath and let it out slowly. *"We still need to get in through the door. We might be able to fry it, but we don't know how strong the insulation is. We might be strong enough to blast it all away; they reckon we're the strongest pair. Or maybe if we combine our power, we can do it."*

"Maybe." He rubbed his chin. *"But we can't test it without giving*

ourselves away."

"No. And we will need to get hold of some clothes. We'll stand out too much with what we're wearing."

The trainees weren't the only people in this place wearing black, but we were the only ones wearing these suits.

I wondered where we could find some suitable uniforms. I assumed they would be stored somewhere within Katoa Labs; it seemed to be pretty self-contained.

"We'll need to switch clothes with a couple of workers once we're in the service corridors." He stared at nothing, thinking hard. *"That might be tricky. We have no idea what their shifts are or when there would be someone in there."*

"A shift timetable would be handy."

But I wasn't sure how we could get hold of something like that. We needed someone who could get into places we couldn't... Someone who could walk through walls...

"What about Allador? He can go anywhere. He might be able to help us. I've tried to call him lots of times, but he still won't answer. I'm worried about him. We haven't heard from him for a long time. I hope he's alright."

"Yeah. I've been worried about him too. What if we try to call him now?"

I frowned. *"I don't know if it will work."*

"We could combine our power to try to find him."

"That could work."

We sat facing each other and held hands. Concentrating was hard as I was still riled up about what Xander had done to me, but we finally managed to join our power together as it flowed through our bodies. We didn't need to create a ball of energy in the air, so we kept the power inside.

We called out to Allador a few times, with no response.

Just as I gave up hope of getting any kind of answer, the room lit up and I opened my eyes to see Allador floating near the doorway.

CHAPTER 41
The Council of Elders

"Allador! It's so good to see you," I said.

He hovered closer and inclined his head. *"Greetings, Lennina. Greetings, Daniel."*

Daniel smiled. *"It's been a while since we've seen you. We were worried about you."*

Allador fluttered around a little. *"I have been forbidden to come to you or to answer your calls. The Elders are not happy. The destruction of our home and food source continues and they are speaking of retaliation against the humans. We are a peaceful race, so this is very disturbing."*

Daniel's face went pale. *"Retaliation? Please, tell them not to hurt anyone. The humans in the tunnels are just doing their jobs and don't even know you exist. It's the leaders of the mining company up here on the space station who know you're there now. We need to get them to stop the mining. Hurting the workers will not stop the company. They will just replace those people."*

"We do not wish to harm anyone, but the situation is dire. The Ampari cannot stand by and let this happen. We need to act."

He seemed to radiate sadness and it seeped into my soul.

Daniel leaned forward. *"Can we talk to the Elders? We need to make them understand."*

Allador fluttered around again. *"I can try. They may not respond."*

His light burned brighter for a few long seconds before he announced they would join us. I was drawn into a Mind-link more powerful than anything I could create and sensed the presence of many minds, including Daniel and Allador.

"These are the members of the Council of Elders," Allador said. *"They*

will speak to you. Elders, these are the humans that wish to stop the destruction."

Daniel got straight to it after we'd said our greetings. *"The equipment the humans used to scan and survey the planet before they started mining could not detect your life forms — only an unknown energy that interfered with their electronics — so they assumed the planet was uninhabited. We have laws in place to protect you as the inhabitants of the planet and mining would have to stop if you don't agree to it."* He repeated what he'd said to Allador about the people in charge being the ones we needed to stop. I could sense anger in the group as he spoke. Daniel stressed that the workers were not the ones to blame. *"I was one of those workers and we were not told of your presence down on the planet. I had no idea until Allador appeared in the tunnel and tried to warn me of the earthquake."*

One of the many minds answered. I couldn't tell which one. They seemed to all blend into one. *"This information is not helpful. How can you make your superiors stop? How do you make them listen to a lowly worker?"*

"I'm not sure how, but we won't give up. And hurting innocent people will not make them stop."

"We will do what is necessary."

Daniel persisted. *"The solution may not lie with the mining company itself, but higher authorities from other planets will make sure this is resolved and the mining stopped. We just need to contact the higher authorities."*

This didn't do anything to gain their confidence, but it was true. The Company wouldn't give up mining that easily as there was too much money to be made, but the authorities from Starfleet Federation would force them to stop all operations.

We'd have to get the word out to Adamo or Daniel's father. They would be able to contact the right authorities.

"We have to force the company to abide by our laws," I told them. *"The higher authorities will force the mining company to stop mining and to open communications with you in regard to mining on your planet."*

"We will speak to only you," one of the Elders told us.

Daniel's eyebrows rose. *"Okay. Umm, yes. They will have to agree to that if they want to negotiate with you. But I'm not qualified..."*

"It matters not. We only speak with you and Lennina."

"Yes, okay."

Allador turned to us. *"We have tried to speak to other humans. You are the first to respond."*

It must have had something to do with our telepathic ability. *"We will try our best to help you,"* I said.

"There is also the problem of the device," the other Ampari voice said.

"What device?" I asked quickly.

"The device the humans have built underground on the planet. We have been observing and listening and the device is meant to destroy us."

CHAPTER 42

You Were Meant to be Together

I gasped. *"We have to stop them!"*

"Do you know how it will destroy you? Do you know what it is?" Daniel asked. *"I can't imagine them using a bomb in the mines. It would destroy the tunnel system."*

"We know not. It is surrounded by an electromagnetic field. We cannot breach this field."

My stomach churned. Katoa were planning to kill the Ampari?

The fact they had built a device to destroy the Ampari meant Katoa had known about the Ampari long before Allador approached Daniel in the tunnels.

I turned to Daniel. *"They've been planning this a long time..."*

Daniel closed his eyes for a few moments.

This was bad. We had to help them, but we couldn't do anything until we could get out of here. We had to enact our plan now.

Daniel looked into my eyes. He knew what I was thinking. *"We'll go as soon as possible."*

My attention was drawn back to the conversation. A few of the Ampari still weren't happy. They were convinced the humans wouldn't listen. They'd tried many times to communicate with the men that were digging in the tunnels, but none of them would acknowledge their existence unless they saw them. Then they'd run.

I tried to tell them that the others couldn't hear them. Allador backed me up.

They finally ended our Mind-link and we were left alone with Allador. *"They are not all happy,"* he told us. *"They will discuss."*

We couldn't wait for that. We had to act before any miners were hurt or Katoa went through with their plan.

He fluttered around. *"I have caused trouble with the Elders."*

I gave a snort. *"So have we."*

He hovered closer to me. *"You are different. Have potential."*

I sucked in a breath. *"What do you mean?"*

He pointed to his head, then pointed to mine. *"Can I touch?"*

I nodded. He reached out and touched my forehead. I sensed his presence in my mind and tried not to squirm as it reminded me of Xander invading my memories. I had to push my anger aside.

It seemed like he was searching around in there. I felt a faint hum, almost like the one I felt whenever I touched Daniel. Could it be the same sort of connection?

"You are different. You have a strong mind. You share Connection with Daniel. No one else."

"Yes. But we don't know how or why."

"Connection initiated on first contact. Connection sealed on first kiss. You are Connected."

He made it sound so... alien. Like we weren't even human. *"But, how? Did you do this to us?"*

"No. I did not do this. This is the Lightning. Something in DNA. You were meant to be together. You were made that way."

I looked across to Daniel. He was staring at me, open-mouthed. I guessed my expression mirrored his. *"But who made us this way? It's not normal for humans."*

"I do not know."

I couldn't help feeling disappointed. I was hoping Allador might have some answers.

He moved away from me and the warmth faded.

I looked up at him. *"We really need to get out of here if we have any hope of helping your people. We have a plan — sort of — but we don't have all the details worked out yet."*

We told him what we'd come up with so far.

"I can help. I can find these workers you seek and I can light your way. When will you be needing me?"

Daniel leaned forward. *"Tomorrow. We'll call you beforehand so you know when we're getting ready. We can't wait any longer. If The Company plan to wipe out your people, we need to act before it's too late."*

Allador inclined his head. *"Many thanks, Daniel. Lennina. I will leave now, and will wait to hear from you."*

We said our goodbyes and once he'd left, I fell into Daniel's open arms. Maybe we could do this. Maybe we could get out of this prison and maybe we could save an alien race from genocide.

──── ★·☆·★ ────

"Come to the entrance now. The humans are on their way."

After a long and sleepless night, we'd bided our time till after lunch, then called Allador to get things started. He'd knocked our guards unconscious and used Raynar's thumbprint to open the door. After disabling the cameras for us, we hid Raynar and Baudin in our bathroom. Once Allador had gone into the service corridor, it hadn't taken him long to find a couple of workers.

We headed toward Lysander's office and when we rounded the corner, the service door was halfway open. I looked around quickly. There was no one in the hallway, so we went in and Daniel slid the door closed so it wouldn't draw the attention of passersby.

The service corridor was a stark contrast to the rest of the station. The walls and ceiling were a dirty-looking, off-white colour and pipes lined the wall opposite the door. The floor was bare and looked like it was made from polished concrete, but I doubted they'd use concrete on a space station. Lights were spaced at regular intervals, so we wouldn't need Allador to light the way.

Two men appeared in the corridor about twenty metres away, dressed in dark blue overalls and walking quickly. They looked nervous, and when they saw us, they sped up.

Allador rounded the corner a few moments later and they looked back apprehensively, but kept coming.

Daniel greeted them and they both started talking at once, telling us the Ghosts were real.

"We know," he told them, "but they're not hostile."

Daniel quickly explained the situation with the device and asked the two men for their help.

The taller man rubbed his chin. "How do we know they're tellin' the truth?"

"We know this Ghost personally," Daniel said, gesturing to Allador. "His name is Allador and after I'd been injured in the collapse down on the planet a few weeks ago, he healed me."

Their eyes widened.

The shorter man with long hair tied back in a ponytail sucked in a breath. "I thought I'd seen yer face before. You was on the news reports."

"Yes. I was messed up pretty badly with broken bones and internal injuries, but I'm fine now. We're short on time. Will you help us get out of here?"

Their smiles faded. "No. Sorry," the tall one said. "We could get in all sorts of strife if we did that. We don't wanna lose our jobs."

Daniel tried a few more times, but it was clear that they wouldn't change their minds.

I noticed them looking at each other nervously and inching away from us, so I gave them enough of a zap to render them unconscious.

Daniel turned to me and I shrugged. "They weren't gonna help us."

He sighed. "I know. Let's take their overalls and find somewhere to put them so they can't rat us out."

The taller guy was a close match with Daniel, but the shorter guy's clothes were too big for me. I rolled the sleeves and pant legs up, but I looked ridiculous.

Daniel giggled. "That'll have to do. Let's go."

Allador used telekinesis to lift both men and put them in a small storage room he'd found earlier. Daniel found some cables to tie their hands and feet together.

Now we had to hurry. *We wasted too much time trying to convince those guys to help,* I said. *Maybe we should have just zapped them as soon as we saw them.*

We had to give them the chance. It would have been quicker and a lot easier to get their clothes if they were conscious.

He was right. He had to help me get the overalls off the guy because he was so heavy. It occurred to me that I should have used some telekinesis to move him myself.

Duh.

Sometimes I just didn't think. Or it could be that I still wasn't used to having Talent.

We started to jog and Allador floated ahead to lead the way. We passed many doors leading who-knows-where and the occasional computer terminal. There were tall lockers that I guessed would be full of whatever equipment the maintenance people needed.

How much longer? Someone's gonna find us.

As soon as those thoughts entered my head, the door ahead of us slid open and people dressed in black poured into the corridor.

CHAPTER 43
Shut Your Stupid Mouth

They were armed with laser pistols and stunners, and I assumed that at least some of them would have destabilisers. I braced myself for the effects.

As Daniel and I started firing low-powered Lightning blasts at them, they ducked for cover and a group of them fired their weapons at Allador.

I was busy defending myself, but from what I could see, laser blasts hurt him. I wanted to help, but I had to duck some blasts that were aimed at me.

I felt the effects of a destabiliser, but it was a weak signal. It must have been too far away. We hadn't been able to test how far they reach because we couldn't leave our rooms while using it.

It put me on edge, but I didn't feel sick. I kept using Lightning and telekinesis to push them back and we were holding our own when I heard a noise behind me. I turned to see more people pouring into the corridor.

"Daniel! Allador! There's more behind us! Be careful."

"Got it. You too," Daniel said.

Allador didn't answer.

Sarinda emerged from the first group and headed toward Daniel.

"Daniel, look out! Sarinda's behind you!"

A Lightning blast sailed past me and hit a computer terminal up ahead of us. Sparks flew everywhere.

I instinctively jerked away from the blast and turned around. Xander was standing in front of the second group with a stupid smirk on his face.

It was obviously a warning shot. He'd had time to take me out while I was distracted.

The computer terminal burst into flames and I cringed. That could have been my head.

I sent a blast his way and it hit his shield and dissipated. "Nice try, Lenni."

I readied my shield as I dodged to the side. "Don't call me that!"

I pushed him back a step or two with a burst of kinetic energy and managed to stay on my feet as he returned it.

We pushed and shoved for a while and threw a few loose objects toward each other, but we were pretty evenly matched.

As I dodged a laser blast from behind me, Xander managed to get past my shield and shoved me to the floor. He used kinetic energy to hold me in place and sat on my legs. I tried to move, but I wasn't going anywhere.

He kept his invisible hold on me as he leaned down close to my face. "You'll never win, Lenni. I'm more powerful than you could ever hope to be. I'm the best that's ever been here at Katoa and you'll never be as good. Power is nothing if you don't know how to wield it properly."

"Get off me!"

It was too difficult to use my Talent to push him off. My energy was flagging.

It was hard to hear him over the noise around us so he switched to telepathy. *"No. You need to know that there's no escape from here. Not until you've proven your loyalty to The Company. They can't have you going around sprouting lies about them. It's bad for business."*

"I don't care. I'm leaving and the stuff I'll be saying won't be lies. It's the truth. About how we've been treated. How they're training soldiers to fight using their Talent. And there is *sentient life on Kronos and breathable air."*

"They'll never let you go if you keep that up."

I kept pushing to try to dislodge him. *"I can't stay here. I'm not going to live a lie. And I'm not going to let them destroy the Ampari."*

"What? What do you mean?"

"The Ampari are in danger. The Company is going to use a device to destroy them down on the planet. You should be helping us. Otherwise

it's genocide. They're going to wipe out a whole race of sentient beings."

"Why should I care about a bunch of aliens?"

My fists clenched. "Why am I bothering trying to explain this to you? You're an imbecile."

"Watch what you say. I'm the one who has you pinned to the floor. And I'm the one who knows all your secrets."

Anger welled up inside me and I pushed with my Talent. He must have anticipated it because he hardly moved.

"Nice try. I know your Daddy would be proud."

"Don't talk about him."

"Why not? Because he walked out on you? Because you feel like a failure as a daughter? Is that it?"

"Shut up!"

"Your father left you because you were a big disappointment."

"I said shut up! You don't know anything about it."

He hadn't seen the memory of what my mother had said about the real reason my father had left us.

"But I do. I've seen it all in your head. Your mother is a lazy sod. She should have tried harder to look after her kids." I tried to push harder against him and his hold started to slip. "You were a hopeless mother to your brother. What made you think you could help raise a kid? You were a kid yourself."

"Keep your trap shut! You know nothing."

He reached into a pocket and pulled out a destabiliser. "This will hold you in place."

Before I could say anything, he pressed the button and I immediately felt the effects. "Idiot. It affects you too."

"Yeah, but I'm physically stronger, so you ain't going nowhere."

He was right. I couldn't push him off.

"I've seen it in your mind. You're pathetic. You don't love Daniel. It's only the Lightning Connection. There's nothing else. You only *think* it's love. We would have been so good together. We're the most powerful."

I wriggled under him, hoping to somehow shift his weight and maybe get out of his trap. "Not this crap again. I don't want to pair with you. It's not possible anyway."

It was hard to hear each other again, but we couldn't speak telepathically with the destabiliser on.

His face was becoming paler. All I had to do was wait till he threw up and I could get the upper hand.

"Maybe if Javolo was out of the way. That could work. But what would Digger Boy think if he knew how you responded when I kissed you? You liked it. I know you did. You want to be with a real man. You want someone more intelligent than a grunt. He's only a Digger because he's too dumb to get a better job."

"Shut your stupid mouth."

"You wish you'd met me first. I know you do. We could have bonded and you'd be having our baby. Our baby would be something we could be proud of. It would help with Katoa's research and we could demand more money because we'd be making more money for them. The sky's the limit. We could do anything."

"You're delusional."

"What makes you think you're better than me? You're such a stuck-up bitch. You think you're better than all of us. You expect special treatment. Well, you don't deserve it. You're nothing special. Sarinda can even kick your arse, and she's only a T3."

I gave up trying to talk to him. I needed to concentrate on resisting the effects of the destabiliser while it made Xander sick.

I zoned out a bit until the nausea faded, and when I heard him talking again, I wanted to punch him.

"Malvolio was trying to help you and you turned him away."

"What part of 'he assaulted me and gave me three broken ribs' did you not understand?"

He gagged a little, but I couldn't make him budge. "You probably did something to deserve that."

"You're an arsehole."

His face was sweating and he looked a bit green. The destabiliser was definitely affecting him a lot more than it was me. Good. I had to keep waiting it out.

"You're so afraid of losing Daniel. You're such a pathetic loser. I can make that a reality for you. I'll turn this thing off and zap him so hard you won't even be able to identify the charred remains."

Panic seized me. *"No!"*

Xander laughed and turned toward Daniel, finger ready to press the button. Mind ready to kill.

NO!

CHAPTER 44

He Was Gonna Kill You

Without even thinking, I threw the energy that had been building inside me from all his insults and watched him fly backwards away from me. He must have pressed the button just after I'd blasted him because the force suddenly increased as I released it. He hit the wall with a sickening crunch and fell in an awkward position.

No, no, no.

The nausea hit me full force as I looked at Xander's twisted form and I turned and threw up on the floor.

Oh, my stars! I've killed him!

I crawled away from my mess as Daniel ran toward me. There didn't seem to be anyone around.

He's dead.

Daniel reached me and helped me to my feet. *"Lennina. We need to go. Now."*

"But... Xander." All I could do was point at him.

He looked over to Xander and grimaced. *"We still need to get out of here."*

"But I think I killed him!"

"I know. I'm sorry. But if we don't go now, we'll *be dead. I don't think they're gonna let us get away. They'll do anything to stop us."*

I turned away from Xander and we ran down the hallway looking for Allador.

I didn't know what to say. The fact that I may have killed someone was too much.

Daniel grabbed my hand. *"It's okay. You're okay."*

"No. I'm not. I... killed him."

"He may be still alive. They may be able to heal him. You'll be okay. I'll make sure of it."

"He... he was gonna kill you."

He glanced my way as we ran. *"He gave you no choice then. You were protecting me. But you can't think about it too much now. I'm not dismissing your feelings. It's just that we have to keep going. You have to be able to function now. We'll have to deal with it later — together — when we're away from danger. Okay?"*

"Okay."

I tried to pull myself together and wiped the tears out of my eyes with the back of my hand so I could see where I was going.

We finally found Allador floating near a doorway that I hoped was the way out of Katoa Labs. He wasn't doing well; there were dark spots on his body, like his light was going out.

"Allador! Are you okay?"

He inclined his head. *"I will be fine, Lennina. I am healing. Keep going."*

He'd already fried the locking mechanism so Daniel slid the door open with his mind and we raced through. We were in a corridor that looked like it belonged on the space station. No pipes on the walls. Nicely painted walls and ceiling and a smooth floor.

I turned back to see Allador using his mind to close the door behind us as we slowed to a walking pace.

I tried to calm my breathing and act like we were just walking toward our next job, but if someone were to look closely, they'd see what a terrible state we were in. I tried to smooth my hair, but it probably didn't make any difference.

After a couple of turns, we entered an area that looked like a shuttle bay. Daniel looked around and headed over to an unusually tall man who was checking things off on a list on his Palm-pad. I couldn't take my eyes off his extremely long, white-blonde hair that was tied back in a ponytail. I wondered if he was from the planet Shakira. The description fitted, but they were a warrior race. It was unusual to find one in a non-military position.

The man looked up and his dark eyes widened. "Hey, Javolo!

Where've you been? I thought you'd gone home."

"Sharwok. Hi. It's a long story. You got a minute?" Daniel gestured for the man to follow and he fell into step with us.

"What's the story?"

"Not here. Where can we talk?"

Sharwok pointed to a nearby door. "In that office. It should be empty."

He let the scanner read his retina and we followed him in.

Daniel started by saying that we needed a lift down to Kronos.

"What for? And where have you been? It's been like, a month or two since I seen ya."

"We've been in training. Like I said. A long story. But we need to get to the planet urgently. Can you get us down to the surface? The fate of a whole species depends on it."

His eyebrows drew together. "Now you're not making any sense. What species? Those things that look like sheep?"

"No. There is a race of sentient beings down there that The Company don't want us to know about."

"How can there be? The whole planet was scanned before they even started mining."

"I know, but these guys can't be found using the usual equipment. They're made out of pure energy and light."

"What?"

"They're called the Ampari and they are the inhabitants of Kronos and they want the mining to stop."

It occurred to me that Allador hadn't followed us into the shuttle bay.

"I am nearby, Lennina. Do not worry."

"Okay."

Daniel and Sharwok spoke for a while longer while Sharwok tried to get his head around the fact that there was life on Kronos, then Daniel told him how badly injured he'd been and that Allador had healed him.

Sharwok looked at Daniel like he'd just told him Kronos was flat. I could see him processing all the information.

He looked Daniel up and down. "And you don't have any injuries now?"

"No. I'm completely fine."

He looked like he needed to sit down. Then he finally asked who I was.

"This is my Nav, Lennina Callista. Lennina, this is Sharwok. I've forgotten your first name. Sorry, man."

"That's okay. It's Baylan."

At least I wasn't the only one to forget first names. I gave him a smile as I said hello.

Daniel turned to him. "So can you help us get down to the planet?"

He rubbed his chin. "I can try. But why do you wanna go down to the planet? To say thank you?"

I fidgeted while Daniel explained things as briefly as he could. About our Talent, but not the Lightning. How we were being trained, but not allowed to go home. How we escaped and now The Company wanted to wipe out a whole race of sentient beings, just so they could continue mining. Thinking about it was enough to make me feel sick.

Daniel stepped closer. "Did you know there's breathable air on Kronos?"

Sharwok gasped. He was clearly shocked. "*What?* No! I don't believe ya."

Daniel put a hand on Sharwok's shoulder. "Believe it. I don't know how or why, but there is. I found out first-hand. When I was injured, my suit sprung a leak."

His eyes went wide. "That's a death sentence!"

"No, it's not. It had a slow leak and I ran out of air completely before Rescue found me."

I shuddered at the memory and fought the threat of tears.

"You're pulling my leg."

Daniel smiled. "No. I couldn't work it out at first — why I was still able to breathe — but when I realised there was air coming in, I popped my shield off and I could breathe easier. The air is too thin — you can't be without a mask for too long — but it's not toxic."

Sharwok looked from Daniel to me and back again. "But why would Katoa lie about something like that?"

Daniel ran a hand through his hair. "I don't know. Maybe there is something down there they don't want us to see."

After thinking about it and much pacing and chin rubbing, Sharwok finally agreed to help us. He walked us to the far end of the shuttle bay and helped us crawl into a large, empty container on one of the pallets before loading it into a shuttle. He rigged the door so it didn't close properly, so we weren't sealed in without oxygen. "Stay here till I can get you some masks."

My heartbeat sped up until I thought it would rattle its way out of my chest. We were actually doing this.

CHAPTER 45
Why Would They Lie?

Hiding in amongst the cargo was nerve-wracking. Although our hiding place seemed quite secure, I expected to be discovered at any minute. I'd never done anything like this before. My legs were jelly and my hands were trembling as we sat in the cramped space.

Sharwok brought us a couple of masks and air tanks and Daniel made sure I knew how to use them properly, then Sharwok sealed us in and went back to his duties. The mask was made of clear Perspex and covered my whole face. As I put it on, it made a sucking sound around the outside edge of my face as it sealed itself, then started delivering air through the tube under my chin.

We were jostled about as we were taken aboard the shuttle, then all was quiet for a few minutes.

The shuttle started its engines and Daniel took my hand.

The engine noises grew louder as we lifted off. The rumbling and vibrations lasted for about a minute, then died down.

Daniel held my hand a little tighter. *"We're in space now. It'll take about ten minutes to reach Kronos's atmosphere."*

This was all new to me, but it was just another day for Daniel; he'd been down to the planet nearly every day for more than a year — except for the part where we were hiding inside a shipping container.

It seemed like such a long wait as we travelled to the surface and I was shaking all over. Daniel put an arm around me and rubbed my shoulder. *"It's okay. It's a short trip. Don't worry."*

The buzzing gave me comfort and the shaking subsided.

The flight was rough as we travelled through the atmosphere and then the sound of the engines changed.

"Sounds like we're touching down," Daniel said. *"Not long now."*

We waited.

Once we'd landed, we heard a loud, muffled voice. Daniel told me it was the standard announcement telling all personnel to put their masks on before the hatch opened.

When Sharwok finally opened the container, he'd brought another unusually tall guy with dark skin and black curly hair with him. My breath caught. He was going to turn us in.

Sharwok smiled warmly. "Hey, Javolo. You know Damaris. He's gonna drive us to the site."

I sighed and tried to slow my racing heartbeat.

"Thanks, Sharwok. Hey, Damaris." Daniel shook both their hands.

"Hi," Damaris said as he nodded to us both. "I can get ya to the place where they're doin' all the new work, but we'll only be here till eighteen hundred, so ya need to be back by then, 'kay?"

"Okay."

Sharwok ran a hand over his face. "I'll come with and try to have a look at this device. I might be able to disable it before they can use it."

Daniel shook his hand again. "Thanks, mate. I appreciate it."

Damaris cleared his throat. "Are you sure there's air here? I mean, why would they lie?"

Daniel responded by pressing the button to disengage the suction around his mask and taking it off.

Damaris and Sharwok gasped and visibly cringed, but Daniel took in a few lungfuls of air to show them it was breathable.

"It's too thin, but there's enough to keep you alive. And it's not toxic at all."

Damaris rubbed his chin. "Well, I'll be damned. I never woulda believed it if I didn't see it for meself."

Daniel put his mask back on and took some more deep breaths. "For people to live down here, they'd have to wear masks while outdoors and have air piped into each building, or they'd need to terraform the planet."

Sharwok looked around. "Right. Yes. We need to get going. Damaris will drive and it won't raise any suspicion if I ride with him. We'll seal you back in until we get there, then I'll go with you while Damaris unloads the rest of this lot. We'll meet him back at the same place he drops us off."

I nodded.

"I appreciate this, boys," Daniel said. "You'll be helping save countless lives."

I tried not to cringe when the door was sealed again.

As we bumped along in the container, I was struck by a terrible feeling of foreboding. It must have been written on my face.

"Lennina? What's wrong?"

I wrapped my arms around my stomach. *"I don't know,"* I told him, *"I just felt... I'm not sure... like we shouldn't go in the tunnels..."*

He put an arm around me again and the buzzing caused warmth to spread through my body.

"It's alright. We'll be okay," he assured me. *"I've been down there hundreds of times before."*

The warmth couldn't quite disperse the cold feeling in my chest. *"Yes, I know, but look what happened the* last *time..."*

The memory of all that pain made me feel worse.

He grimaced. *"Yeah, I know, but we* have *to go in there if we want to find the device, don't we?"*

I sighed. *"Yes."*

"I've been down so many times without a single incident. You know that. You were with me..."

I smiled. I'd been with him every step of the way over the Com system. I'd guided him through the maze of tunnels, making sure he got through to where the deposits were and back to the shuttle again once he'd loaded up with Amakio.

Despite all of that, I couldn't shake the feeling.

Maybe it's fear because I haven't been in the tunnels before.

I shuddered as I imagined us entering the abyss and tried to tell myself I was just being silly.

When we finally stopped moving, I'd almost stopped my brain from conjuring up images of tunnel collapses and being buried alive.

Sharwok let us out and we quickly followed him to an alcove on the edge of a large cavern. "We can start looking around as soon as Damaris leaves to deliver the rest of the cargo."

Daniel and Sharwok's voices faded away and the dirt walls of the tunnel loomed in front of me and I was taken back to the hole in the ground and the dirt and tree roots that seemed to surround and engulf my six-year-old self. I could almost see the insects crawling over my feet and I shuddered. It was so real.

I tried to ground myself by looking at the buggy with the trailer full of containers that had brought us here, but it didn't help when the dirt surrounded me on three sides.

Daniel turned to me. "Lennina? Are you okay?"

CHAPTER 46
That's Spaced, Man

"Umm... I..." My breathing was shallow and my heart pounded loudly. I couldn't form the words.

"What's wrong?"

Sharwok turned to Daniel. "What's going on?"

I swayed a little. I was light-headed and couldn't get my breathing under control.

Daniel helped me to sit on the ground, which didn't help because the dirt was what I needed to escape from. "She's having a panic attack. She needs a moment."

"That's just great. That's all we need. We need to hurry this up before someone sees us."

"I know. Just hold on." Daniel put his arms around me. *"Lennina? It's okay. I've got you. You're alright. Just breathe. Slower, deeper breaths."* He rubbed my back and the little circles calmed me. *"Try to relax."*

I concentrated on the sensations running through me at his touch, as well as the Lightning's buzz. After a few minutes, the symptoms subsided enough for me to stand. "Sorry."

"No need to apologise," Daniel said. "Are you okay now?"

"I think so. Being underground triggered a memory of falling down a hole in the ground when I was six. I was trapped there overnight with bugs crawling over me." I shuddered.

Sharwok grimaced. "You should have told us this before you came down here. You're no good to us if you're gonna faint at every turn."

Daniel gave him a look. "Go easy on her, man."

"We need to get moving. We have to have all this done before the shuttle leaves."

"I know," I said. "I'm sorry."

Although I still wasn't feeling well, we set off and I kept my focus on Sharwok's boots as he walked ahead of us and I tried not to think about that hole in the earth.

Sharwok took us through the tunnels towards the place where there had been some new activity and stopped every now and then to mark our position on a small digital device that Damaris had given us. Now I didn't have to worry about us getting lost. Daniel kept an eye on the time and an eye on me.

I couldn't help it. I had to ask. "What is that device? I thought GPS guidance didn't work at all down here."

Sharwok held it up so I could see. "It's new technology and we only have a few devices. It is able to filter out most of the interference that's coming from the planet, so we have limited navigational capabilities."

"That's great. Maybe they will get more of them."

It occurred to me that it wouldn't matter once we'd stopped the mining.

Daniel turned to me. "Do you think we could get Allador to show us where the device is?"

"Yes."

I'd been wondering where he'd gone and hoped he was somewhere down here on the planet.

"Allador? Are you nearby?"

Daniel turned to Sharwok. "We're gonna call one of the aliens to help us find the device."

Sharwok looked uneasy. "Okay."

"Lennina? I am near."

"Can you come here? We have someone with us who's going to try to disable the device."

"If you wish."

Even though I was anticipating the bright light, it still had to hold a hand up to shield my eyes.

Sharwok gasped and Daniel told him that it was okay.

"Hello, Allador," I said. "This is Sharwok. He wants to help."

Allador nodded to each of us. *"Greetings."*

Sharwok gasped again. "I can hear him talking in my head!"

I was surprised that he could hear Allador. Maybe he had some Talent. Maybe it was because he was open to it.

"Yes," Daniel said. "The Ampari communicate using telepathy. Lennina and I were the first people to actually hear them."

Sharwok looked at Daniel in awe. "That's spaced, man." He turned to Allador. "Can you show us where this device is?"

Allador nodded. *"Follow me."*

We fell in behind Allador as he floated through the tunnels. There was no need for the lights that were built into our masks as he lit up the whole area.

As we were about to enter another open area, Allador stopped. *"This is as far as I can go. I cannot breach the electromagnetic field surrounding the device without causing myself much harm."*

"Okay. Thank you, Allador," Daniel said. "We'll have a look and see if we can stop this thing."

Allador inclined his head. *"Many thanks, Daniel."*

As we walked forward, it was like stepping into a room where someone had switched on a destabiliser.

I hesitated. "Daniel? Can you feel that?"

He turned to me. "Yes. The destabilisers must work by emitting an electromagnetic field."

It wasn't as strong as a destabiliser when it was up close and directed at me, but it was definitely the same sort of sensation.

Sharwok turned back. "What is it?"

"We can feel the effects of the field around the device," Daniel said.

"How? It's not affecting me."

"It's part of that long story I told you about."

Sharwok frowned. "Okay. Does it mean you have to turn back?"

"No, man. It's just making us feel on-edge. We're good. Let's go."

We walked toward a metallic device that was about the size of a small wardrobe and the feeling didn't get any worse. That was a relief. I was again thankful that we had increased our tolerance.

Sharwok got to work immediately and opened a panel on the side.

He pulled out a small device from a compact backpack he'd brought with him. "This interface has all the ports on it that Katoa uses for their equipment. One of them should fit this thing."

I sighed. Maybe we could do this without too much trouble.

We waited as he found the correct port and tapped away on the interface's screen.

He ran a hand through his hair. "This looks like an EMP device. Built to send an electromagnetic pulse through the tunnels, I presume. It is sophisticated, but I think I'll be able to shut it down. It's just a matter of tracking down a few things..."

Daniel sighed. "That's great, mate. What do you need us to do?"

"Stand guard, I guess. I need to be able to concentrate on what I'm doing and not worry about what The Company could possibly do to stop us if they discover what we're doing."

I shuddered to think of what that might be. Surely there'd be cameras down here so they could keep an eye on this thing. Once they saw us down here, they'd have to send someone to at least see what we were doing.

I looked around, but couldn't see any obvious cameras.

We stood with our backs to Sharwok, watching for any movement within the cavern or from the three tunnels that led into it.

Time dragged on and my mind conjured up too many disturbing scenarios involving people from Katoa or security from Katoa Labs running at us from all three tunnels and had to push those thoughts aside. They were not helping.

How long is this gonna take?

I fidgeted and tried to concentrate.

Daniel glanced back over his shoulder. "How's it going there, Shar? We need to book it as soon as you're done."

"It's more complicated than I thought," he said. "Just a bit longer, I think."

I resisted the urge to sigh. It wouldn't help Sharwok feel any better.

"Lennina, can you pass me that little black cylindrical thing in my backpack with the pointed tip, please?"

I found what he was referring to and held it up. "You mean the non-contact voltage tester?"

"Oh, yeah. Sorry. I didn't realise you knew what it was."

I passed it to him. "That's okay."

"Hello, Lennina, my love."

CHAPTER 47

I Can't Let You Ruin My Plans

My stomach dropped as I spun around. Malvolio had entered through one of the tunnels opposite where we'd come in.

"I'm not your love!" I snapped.

Daniel stepped forward. "What are you doing here?"

"I could ask you the same thing." He turned to Sharwok. "I'd stop fiddling around with that device if I were you."

I glanced at Sharwok, who went straight back to work. He sniffed. "Who are you to be telling me what to do?"

Malvolio straightened his shoulders. "I'm The Company."

I thought I must've been hearing things. "What?"

"Listen very carefully," he said slowly, as if I had a diminished mental capacity. "I. Am. The. Fucking. Company. It's me. I own it. I'm not just the managing director in charge of Galaxy Mech, I am the owner of Katoa Intergalactic Mining and Exploration. It's all mine."

He looked proud of himself and my stomach sank. No wonder he had been allowed to be involved in every aspect of our testing and training.

"So you see, you *do* need to do as I say."

I'd seen that darkness in his eyes before and I cringed inwardly. He was a dangerous man when he wanted to be.

Sharwok stopped what he was doing, but kept one hand on the device, the other near the screen on his interface. He wasn't going to give up so easily.

"I don't understand," I said. "You know about the Ampari—"

"The what?"

"The Ampari. The aliens. The rightful owners of the planet you're mining."

"Not for long."

I tried not to react to that. "So like I said, I don't understand. If you own Katoa, then this device—"

"Is ready to go. It's all been calculated. We need to send an electromagnetic pulse, combined with a laser light calibrated to the right settings, through the tunnel network, to put it in simple terms. My scientists have tested it on a few individuals and assure me that that will knock the pests on the head. Then we will be free of them and their interference to all our electrical systems."

They had already killed some of them? I scowled at him. "They are sentient beings, not just an interference!"

Daniel stepped forward. "You can't do that!"

"Oh, but I can and I will. It's almost ready... We have most of our equipment stored inside Faraday cages under the surface and we will shut off all other equipment while we do it. It probably won't save them, but that will be acceptable losses. I'll coordinate it all from here..."

I couldn't believe what I was hearing. Was he serious? "But you can't! It's genocide!" I said. "They are a peaceful race! We've been able to communicate with them and you already know that one of them healed us."

"None of that matters."

"We've spoken to their Council of Elders. They explained the situation from their point of view. By mining the Amakio, we are destroying their habitat and stealing their food source. We informed them of their rights in this situation and told them we'd do everything in our power to stop you."

His eyebrows drew together. "There's too much riding on this. I can't let you ruin my plans."

My entire body went cold.

"What plans?" Daniel asked.

"I had plans for this whole planet," Malvolio said. "Once I've removed the Ghosts, all I need to do is keep mining the Amakio until it dries up, which, they tell me, will be in another ten years or so. After that, we will fill in the tunnel systems, terraform the planet and make a fortune by selling the land and establishing big business here. I'll be set for life."

"No!" Daniel said. I'd lost my voice.

Malvolio turned to me. "Pity... You could have shared the glory with me — and the credits. We would've been rich. Rich beyond your wildest dreams — way beyond *your* wildest dreams — especially considering where you've come from... You had a chance to be saved from the gutter, but you chose to return there..." He looked to Daniel as he said it.

"I was never in the gutter," I snapped. "I was perfectly fine until you came along. You ruined everything and now I don't even have my freedom anymore. Well that's all gonna change. We're not going back to your prison again."

"You will!"

"No. Don't forget who you're dealing with. I put you in the Infirmary once already."

Instead of answering, he pulled a destabiliser from his pocket and I managed to not laugh as he pressed the button.

"Now you can't hurt me," he said. "I have the upper hand."

The edgy feeling increased, but the destabiliser didn't affect us the way he'd hoped. Outwardly, we gave the impression that it wasn't affecting us at all, but it was still hard to tolerate.

His eyebrows shot up.

I'd pushed past the effects before when I blasted Xander, so I knew I could do it again. I pushed hard and managed to knock the destabiliser out of his hand.

"What? How did you do that?"

I laughed. "That thing doesn't work on us anymore."

Just to prove my point, I picked it up with my mind and threw it down the tunnel he'd come through.

I saw movement from the corner of my eye as Sharwok typed something on his screen. Before I knew what was happening, a laser blast hit him in the face and sent him flying backward into the wall. He slid down to the floor and slumped forward.

CHAPTER 48

I'm sorry, Allador. We failed

My mind scrambled to catch up as Daniel yelled out and rushed forward to check on his friend.

I turned to see Malvolio holding a laser pistol with a smirk on his face. I couldn't talk. Could hardly breathe.

Daniel let out a sob as he gently laid the big man onto his back. His face was a charred mess within his melted mask. The smell of burnt flesh and melted plastic hit my nostrils and I threw up on the dirt floor.

Malvolio picked up Sharwok's interface and started muttering to himself. I assumed he was trying to undo whatever Sharwok had done to it.

I pushed through the effects of the field. *"Daniel. Let's get out of here while he's busy with that thing."*

Daniel looked up through his tears and nodded. We moved slowly toward the entrance to the tunnel and I cringed, expecting to feel the burn of the laser at any second.

Once we were inside the tunnel, I wrapped my arms around Daniel. I was trembling all over, but I wanted to comfort him. We held each other tight for a few moments, then continued on in case Malvolio decided to follow us.

I cursed the masks. I really needed to kiss him. To try to take some of his pain away.

We kept moving and it felt wonderful to escape the effects of the electromagnetic field.

When I heard a loud hum coming from the cavern, my chest tightened. It probably meant Malvolio had stopped the shutdown.

I could hear Malvolio's voice down the tunnel as he spoke to someone over the Com. He had already initialised the device and was coordinating with other people to initialise the other devices scattered throughout the tunnel system. He was going to do this *now*.

I felt on edge again. The electromagnetic field must have increased when he initialised it.

My heart twisted in my chest. After all our efforts to get here, Sharwok had died in vain. The Ampari were still going to be obliterated. We'd probably end up back at Katoa Labs for the rest of whatever, facing punishment for escaping and maybe for killing Xander.

A sob escaped and I couldn't stop myself from crying. Daniel pulled me into his arms in a little alcove and I let the warmth of his embrace soak into my soul.

We stayed like that for a while as recent events played on a loop in my head. I couldn't get the image of Sharwok's face out of my mind. Why did Malvolio have to shoot him in the face? He could have injured him instead. Could have just threatened him with the gun. That would have stopped him from shutting the device down. Malvolio was a cold-hearted monster.

"What are we gonna do?" I asked.

My anxiety rose when Daniel didn't answer.

There was nothing we could do. The device was almost ready to go.

What would happen when it does? Would the light affect our eyes? Would the electromagnetic pulse affect us too because of our Lightning abilities? Maybe we would die too.

There was no way to help the Ampari.

"I'm sorry, Allador. We failed. We tried so hard. We tried our best, but it wasn't good enough. We can't save you."

"Do not be sad, Lennina. We are grateful for the effort you have made."

More tears streamed down my face. How could he be so calm?

"Allador? Can't your people go to the space station to avoid the pulse?"

"No, Lennina. Not all can go. Some are too weak. Their light is dimming. So none would go."

"But that's suicide."

"It is how it is. We all go, or none go. We won't leave any to die."

"But..."

I had to respect their point of view, even if I didn't agree with it.

The field was getting stronger now. We had to move further away. Using my Talent was becoming more difficult.

"Come on, Daniel. We have to move away from the field."

"Okay."

We started walking again. "I'm sorry about Sharwok."

Daniel nodded.

"We shouldn't have taken him with us. Then he'd still be alive."

Daniel's head snapped to mine. "We couldn't have known Malvolio would do that."

"I know. But..."

Once the effects of the field died away, everything lit up and we saw Allador and three other Ampari floating further down the tunnel. They approached slowly and I noticed that they were different sizes and that some emitted a brighter light than others. I wondered why their light would be dimmer than Allador's when he was still healing.

"Greetings, Lennina. Greetings, Daniel. These are some of my family members. I believe you would call them siblings. We are all suffering with the reduction of our food source in this area."

I gasped. They were slowly starving.

CHAPTER 49
For Them

We greeted the others and Allador told us their names, but my mind was too preoccupied to retain anything. I tried to smile, but it probably looked more like a grimace. Did they know what was about to happen to them?

"You should leave now," Allador said. *"Because of your Lightning Connection and abilities, you may be damaged when the pulse hits, and I won't be here to heal you."*

New tears flooded my eyes at the thought. How could we help them?

I looked at the faces of the smallest of the Ampari and going back to the shuttle was suddenly not an option. We couldn't leave them here to die.

The fate of an entire species was in our hands. If they died, no one would even know they existed outside Katoa Intergalactic Mining and Exploration.

"No," I said. *"We can't go."* Daniel looked at me. *"We can't abandon them."*

He nodded slowly. *"We need to look at our options. The Ampari can't go in there, so we're on our own. We'll have to push harder to use our Talent with the field surrounding the device, but we can do it. We don't know how to disable it, so we need to destroy it. We can try to blast it, but it could cause the cavern to collapse."*

I shuddered at the thought. *"What if one of us creates a shield around the whole area and the other blasts?"*

His eyebrows rose. *"That could work."*

"You can create a stronger shield than I can, so I'll do the blasting."

He smiled. *"You got it."*

When we crept back into the cavern, Malvolio wasn't there. It was just as well with the increased electromagnetic field. Using my Talent was harder than before.

I sucked in a breath when I saw Sharwok's body. I still couldn't believe Malvolio had killed him. It was surreal.

The nausea increased and I had to look away.

Daniel's face was twisted with grief and he turned away too. "We need to be close enough to blast it, but far enough away that we won't be hit by the Lightning or debris."

I walked over to the device. "Wait. What if I could work out how to—"

"There's no time."

He didn't stop me. We had nothing to lose. The panel was open, but Sharwok's interface had been removed. There was no way for me to interact with the device at all.

I sighed. "I had to try."

Daniel squeezed my hand and we looked around for a place to sit while we did this. We didn't know how thick the casing was, so we would have to keep trying until something gave.

Daniel held me for a few moments. "Concentrate the blasts on the panel with the ports. That should be a weak point."

I nodded.

I relished the buzzing sensations caused by our touch as we concentrated on letting the Lightning build up inside us. We had to get this right, or the Ampari would die.

The power building inside me wasn't enough. The electromagnetic field was making it difficult to concentrate. As the power built, so did the nausea, but we had to do this.

As Daniel concentrated on building a shield, I prepared to zap the device.

He created a shield around us first, and the relief was palpable. His shield blocked out the electromagnetic field.

We looked at each other and Daniel nodded.

He expanded the shield as he fed it more energy until it took up most of the cavern. "Okay, start blasting when you're ready."

The energy flowed around my hands and I pushed it straight at the device. When the Lightning dissipated, the area I'd struck was charred, but otherwise the device was unharmed.

I tried a few more times, but it wasn't causing enough damage. "It's not working! The blasts aren't strong enough."

"What's this thing made of?"

I tried to hold back the tears. How could we do this? How could we save them?

Daniel put his hands on my upper arms. "We need to combine our power. Create an energy ball. A big one."

"I'm not sure I can. I'm so worn out."

"We have to try. For them."

I pictured the young Ampari's faces, took a deep breath and nodded. "For them."

I tried to ignore the bile rising in my gut and joined hands with Daniel. I closed my eyes.

"Relax. Gather your energy. Concentrate on my voice."

It was difficult, but I used Daniel's voice and the physical contact to ground me. I sensed the shield drop and had to block out the feelings of edginess and nausea and concentrated harder.

I built up the energy and pushed it outward.

When I opened my eyes, the ball of energy floating in the air was bigger than any of the ones we'd created back at Katoa Labs.

Daniel's eyes seemed to shine as he looked at me through the energy ball. "Keep going. It needs to be bigger if we're gonna get through that casing."

I nodded and gave it some more power.

He grinned. *"Now I'll let you have the ball and concentrate on making the shield again."*

My energy was draining fast, but we needed to do this.

I pushed my concerns aside. Emptied my mind of all the things that had happened. Daniel passed the power to me and I hoped it wasn't too much for one person to handle.

Daniel needed more energy. More power to create a shield big enough to contain the blast. So I'd have to hold the ball till he was ready.

I kept the ball steady and pushed it above us so we could still hold hands without touching it.

The relief once he'd created the shield again was very welcome. He expanded it and we were ready to roll.

"I need to stand up so I have enough clearance to throw this thing."

We carefully got to our feet without touching the ball and I prepared to push it full force and duck.

"Stop this right now!"

CHAPTER 50
You Can't Stop Me

I jumped and almost lost my hold on the ball. Malvolio had returned and was holding the laser pistol in one hand and a case in the other.

"Keep the ball up!" Daniel said.

I made sure it was steady. "I'd keep back if I were you."

Malvolio smiled. "You need to make that ball disappear. If you try to destroy my machine, I will not hesitate to kill both of you." He made a show of looking at his watch. "We're going to wait here until the machine does its thing. Then I'll be rid of the interference for good."

I squared my shoulders. "You can't do this! It's genocide!"

"You can't stop me. If you try, I'll shoot, and the aliens will still die."

Daniel shifted his weight from one foot to the other. *"What do you wanna do?"*

"I'm gonna blast it. When I tell you to, duck away from him."

"Okay."

Malvolio moved closer. "I told you to get rid of the ball, now do it!"

I looked at Daniel. *"Now!"*

I pushed the ball at the device with as much force as I could and ducked for cover.

Pain struck my left shoulder just before I hit the ground and the explosion hurt my ears. I hoped we'd finally penetrated the casing.

My shoulder was agony. Had some of the energy bounced back at me somehow? Was it a piece of shrapnel from the explosion?

I looked around and was happy to see the device in twisted, charred pieces spread over a wide area.

I felt my shoulder as I looked down and my heart sank as I found nothing there — that meant Daniel was hurt.

Before I'd even thought about it, I was crawling over to where he was lying on the ground. *"Daniel? Are you okay?"*

He coughed. *"Not exactly."*

"What happened?"

"Laser blast."

Oh, no!

His overalls were charred and I could see how bad it was. I could *feel* how bad it was. Those black suits weren't able to stop a laser burn.

Oh, this is not good.

He needed medical attention, and soon.

He looked up at me. *"Are you okay? You're bleeding."*

"Where?"

"Your arm."

I followed his gaze. There was blood trickling down my left arm from under my sleeve. I felt my arm till I found a sore spot below my elbow. I hadn't even noticed the pain.

I pushed the sleeve up and my fingers found something sharp. There was a piece of shrapnel in my arm. I took a deep breath and pulled it out. The pain hit and I could feel a few more wounds across my back. I held up the piece. It was about the size of my thumbnail. *"A piece of the device."*

"Did we stop it?"

I grinned. *"Yes. There's pieces everywhere and the EM field is gone."*

He smiled, then grimaced.

My smile disappeared. I didn't have to ask him how bad it was; I was having trouble blocking out his pain. Something we hadn't quite perfected yet, but even if we had, I doubted I could block this much pain.

Malvolio strode across the room.

"What have you done? You could have brought the whole mountain down on us, you imbeciles! You've ruined my device and delayed my plans."

He waved the pistol around as he spoke and I noticed he was uninjured. He must have been standing outside Daniel's shield.

"It will cost me a lot of credits to have it rebuilt — and I *will* have it rebuilt. I will still go ahead with my plan, and you won't be around anymore to stop me."

Before he could fire the pistol and end my life, a group of black-clad people came into the cavern — Sarinda and some security guards from Katoa Labs.

Sarinda strode ahead of the others. "You bitch! You killed Xander!"

My chest tightened. I thought that maybe I had, but to hear her say it...

"Why did you do it? I can't believe you'd do this to me!"

Malvolio looked at her. "Sarinda, he is in the Infirmary being treated for a fractured spine and other internal injuries. He is *not* dead."

Instead of feeling relief, my heart twisted. Why did she have to lie about something like that?

"He's not going to make it." She started to sob, then her face contorted into a mask of hatred. "Why did you hurt him like that? You couldn't have him, so you thought you'd take him away from me?"

I stood on shaky legs. "No! It's not like that. He was gonna kill Daniel! I had to stop him."

"You don't understand! I loved him. There's no one else for me. He was my one true love."

"Stop talking like he's already gone."

"He is. You should see him. He's like a ghost lying there."

"But Malvolio said—"

"*Fuck* what Malvolio said. I know it. I can see it. He's gone."

Without warning, she fired a Lightning blast straight at my chest. It burned and added to the pain I was already in. I was thrown back onto the floor next to where Daniel had propped himself against the wall.

My hastily-created shield stopped the next blast, but she kept firing. It stopped the next few blasts, but she soon tore it down. I curled into a ball as I received the full force of her Lightning power and she screamed in rage.

The pain became unbearable and when it suddenly stopped, it left me stunned and gasping for breath. Daniel had managed to shield me. I couldn't form the words to thank him so I put a hand on his arm, hoping he would understand.

The beautiful rainbow of colours produced by her Lightning strikes as they hit the shield betrayed how deadly they were.

I wasn't sure how long she could keep it up and I feared Daniel wouldn't be able to hold the shield till she stopped.

Finally, she stopped blasting. As soon as she did, Daniel dropped the shield. *"Sorry. I can't... "*

"It's okay," I managed. *"Thank you."*

Sarinda sank to her knees with her hands over her face, sobbing. Malvolio moved closer. The security guards had moved into position, surrounding us on three sides. I counted seven of them, all holding a stunner in one hand and a destabiliser in the other.

I groaned. How were we supposed to fight them off when I was completely drained? I had nothing left to give.

Maybe we could let them take us away so we wouldn't be killed.

Yeah, right. Who was I kidding with Malvolio standing over us with the gun?

Maybe I could try to reason with them.

"We give in," I said. "Take us back to Katoa and we'll go back to training. We'll behave ourselves."

My stomach churned at the thought of going back there and Daniel tensed behind me. *"What are you doing? I thought you never wanted to go back there."*

"Buying us some time."

"Okay."

"That is not a workable solution," Malvolio said.

"We'll do as you say. I'll put more effort into training. I'll even take Dr Lysander seriously."

"It's too late for that. You will never behave. It's not in your nature. You were always a rebel who couldn't follow rules. Pity. You could have had it all." He pointed the gun at Daniel. "So now you can watch your caveman die."

"NO!"

CHAPTER 51

I'm So Sorry, Daniel

I rushed forward, pushing what little energy I could muster at Malvolio as pain tore into the right side of my chest, but the blast had missed me. I turned to see the laser pistol blast a long line that started at Daniel's chest and went up the wall and onto the roof of the cavern before Malvolio released the trigger.

"Daniel!" I screamed.

I gasped as dirt and rocks from the ceiling showered down on us all. There were shouts and cries of pain from everyone as they scrambled toward the tunnel entrance.

I was knocked to my knees as something hit me on the head and it added to the agony of Daniel's injuries.

"Daniel!"

I dropped to my knees and started to crawl back to where he was sitting, but my mind was hazy. Then there was a loud crack and the whole ceiling came down.

My first thought was to protect Daniel. I somehow found the energy to stop the earth landing on him. From there I was able to create a shield that held it all in place.

I breathed a little easier, but I was too weak to be using this much power. I wasn't sure how long I could keep the shield in place.

I realised I'd been squeezing my eyes shut and opened them to total blackness. I felt around in the dark; the rocks above me had somehow formed a small pocket for me to lie in.

For once I was glad I had the mask on. It had stopped me from getting dirt in my eyes and mouth.

It was amazing to me that I'd somehow escaped certain death. What were the chances of the rocks falling the way they did?

But I had to stop wondering how I was still alive and concentrate on the shield.

Had anyone survived besides Daniel and I?

I felt a stabbing pain in my heart; what if he hadn't survived?

"Daniel?"

Nothing.

I had to fight the panic. I took some deep breaths.

With all my effort going into the shield, I wasn't able to block Daniel's pain too, so the fact that I couldn't feel it was adding to my panic. It could have meant that he was unconscious and I refused to think about him being... anything *but* unconscious.

My heart ached. We'd been through so much together and tried so hard to stop the massacre of the Ampari. What if after all of that, he hadn't made it? What would I do?

The tears welled up in my eyes, but I had to push those thoughts aside and concentrate. There was still a chance he was alive. He *had* to be alive. He needed urgent medical attention, or for Allador to heal him again.

Allador!

Where was he? Where were the other Ampari? Did we save them?

"Allador? Are you there?"

"Greetings, Lennina." He sounded exhausted. *"Are you well? Do you need to be healed?"*

"Allador! I'm so glad you're still here. What about the others? Are they okay?"

"Yes, Lennina. My people survived, but many individuals are not well."

My heart sank. We needed to stop the mining, but we had to get out of here first.

A wave of exhaustion hit me and I almost dropped the shield. *"Allador, can you help me?"*

"I am sorry. I am shielding you from harm and do not have more energy to send to your shield."

"Oh. I didn't know. Thank you."

Of course he was shielding me. I'd been silly to think that some kind of miracle had saved me from being crushed.

"How can we get out of here? I can't hold this shield much longer. I have no more energy."

"I have called on others. They will help when they arrive."

"How long? Where did they go?"

"They went away as far as they could, but I fear it would not have been enough in the event of the device being fully activated. We thank you for your efforts in stopping our destruction."

I wanted to smile, but couldn't bring myself to do it.

I was certain neither of us could last much longer and that filled me with a strange kind of sadness. Was I going to die right here? Right now? Was this the end?

Sweat covered my forehead and ran down my back from the exertion. I couldn't do it. I was getting weaker.

It was getting harder to breathe and a hissing sound meant there was a hole in my mask. I hadn't noticed the sound before. It must have been damaged by a falling rock. A soft beeping sound told me the tank had run out of air, so I disengaged the mask and took it off. Of course it didn't make it much easier to breathe...

I was losing this battle. My energy was almost gone.

I thought about my life. I was twenty years old and hadn't really lived. The only exciting thing I'd ever done was to travel off-world to work for Katoa, and that hadn't entailed visiting any exotic new planets — I'd only seen the inside of the station.

The best thing about coming out here was meeting Daniel.

I thought of our first day working together. I was nervous and didn't want to say anything out of line. It seemed like Daniel was trying to be on his best behaviour, too. He was so stiff and rigid. It was kind of funny now to think back on it. We needn't have worried; we were both such a perfect match for each other. More than we could ever have imagined.

Once we'd gotten our nerves out of the way and discovered we both had the same sense of humour, we picked up the pace and got down to work, bringing in as much Amakio as possible every day. It'd been so much fun...

My brain skipped from one thing to the next. Malvolio hurting me. The first tunnel collapse. Javolo being hurt. Finding out he was Daniel. Kissing him. Watching him being healed. The endless training and the torture. Xander. Escaping and coming down here. Malvolio shooting Sharwok, then Daniel...

They raced through my mind and became jumbled. My head throb bed...

Then things started to slow down. My mind was fading. I could feel it.

Now my life would all come to an end. Mine and Daniel's. And for what? Everything seemed so meaningless if it was to end right now...

Tears flowed freely from my closed eyes and I brought my knees up to my chest, curling into a ball. It didn't help. It didn't magically give me the extra strength I needed to carry on.

Everything kept rolling through my mind. *It can't end like this...*

I waited and clung to the small hope that someone would be looking for us, or even for Malvolio, but help didn't come. I was becoming desperate. I couldn't keep it up. Sooner or later, I would have to let go. I would have to let Daniel die.

Allador was still calling for help from his kind and I heard the panic in his voice in my mind, but nothing... No one...

I tried so hard, but couldn't hold on any longer. My heart was aching. I felt the shield slipping from my tenuous grasp. I held on a bit longer. Rocks started to fall through the shield. I saw them in my mind's eye. Could hear them nearby. One of them hit Daniel's leg. *I'm so sorry, Daniel... I love you...*

The darkness was there. It was calling to me. I was so exhausted. Sweat covered me. My body trembled with the exertion. There was no way to avoid it. The rocks were slipping. My mind was slipping. I was sliding into unconsciousness.

My last thought before the blackness took me was, *I've let him die...*

CHAPTER 52
Are You Not Happy?

Consciousness came swirling back. Something wasn't quite right. As feeling returned to my body, I felt that I was lying on a hard, lumpy surface.

For some reason, it was hard to breathe. My brain struggled to remember what had happened and where I was. Opening my eyes to darkness didn't help. Where was I?

I was lying on my left side in an awkward position and couldn't remember how I'd gotten there. There was dirt beneath me. That explained why I was so uncomfortable.

Think! I told myself, *Focus... Where am I? What's wrong with the air?*

My mind remained foggy but the dirt floor sparked something. The tunnels. The cavern. The device. Malvolio had appeared and — *No!*

It all came flooding back to me. I gasped as I tried to suck more air into my burning lungs.

Daniel.

He'd been crushed. I'd passed out and dropped my shield, but Allador was obviously stronger than me.

Tears welled up in my eyes and I closed them tight as I curled into a tight ball. Daniel was dead. My whole world was crashing down on me. Sobs racked my body as the pain in my heart gripped me. I didn't want to be the one to survive if it meant that he was gone. I'd only just found someone who felt like he was my soul mate, and I'd lost him too soon.

Maybe Allador should've let the rocks fall on me too.

A bright light pierced the darkness, forcing me to shield my eyes. *"Allador?"*

"Yes, Lennina?"

I didn't know what to say. I was happy to know he was still there, and I knew I should be grateful to still be alive, but Daniel hadn't made it.

Why couldn't I have held on longer? I should've tried harder to save him. Guilt cut into my heart like a knife.

"Thank you..."

As my eyes adjusted to the light and I blinked away tears, I saw Allador incline his head in response.

My mind raced. The fact that I could see Allador floating nearby told me that the earth had been moved from above me.

"What happened?"

"The others arrived when you fell. They helped me to lift rocks. It took much energy. We had to move much earth away."

I shifted to a sitting position and looked up. It looked like we were in a massive hole in the ground with a huge patch of sky above us. My head spun. There were millions of stars twinkling out there. It made me feel very small. They'd had to move a *lot* of dirt. *"Thank you."*

How much energy would it have taken to accomplish such a huge task?

More tears fell as I thought about Daniel. My heart was hollow. I knew it was Malvolio that had fired the pistol, but I couldn't shake the guilt for pushing his hand upward and causing the collapse. And for not being strong enough to hold out longer. If I'd been able to hold out even a few seconds more, the Ampari could have saved him. I started to cry again, but it was hard to breathe with the thin air.

"Lennina. Why are you distressed? Are you not happy?" Allador asked.

I couldn't bring myself to stop crying to explain why I was so upset. Would he understand grief over the death of a loved one? Surely they would grieve. They were intelligent beings.

I pulled my knees up to my chest and wrapped my arms around them, rocking myself back and forth on the ground. I didn't care that I was being watched by a growing number of Ampari.

I pictured Daniel's handsome face, then recalled that conversation over the Com.

"Anyway, guess what?"

I smiled. Javolo didn't miss a beat. It was straight back to our con-

versation. "What?"

"Last night I saw the most beautiful woman I've ever seen!" he exclaimed through the static over the Com.

"Ah-huh. Like the redhead you saw last month?" I laughed. "Or the brunette in the grav shaft last week?"

"No," he said quickly, "this is different. Cut me some slack, huh?"

He'd been talking about me...

Despite feeling such an overwhelming sadness, I stopped rocking and smiled. That was how it had always been between us right from the start. I'd dig at him and he would do the same back to me. We'd had such great times together. Why I couldn't see that there was something more than friendship between us, I would never know.

Hey... wait a minute. I wasn't in any pain. I felt my head and the other places I'd been injured. Nothing.

"Yes," Allador told me, *"you are healed."*

"I can't thank you enough," I said simply. *"I thought I was going to die, that we both couldn't hold on forever. I thought no one would come to help..."*

"We help you," he said. *"We need you."*

I was sure there was more to it than that for Allador. He'd risked so much to go up to the station and heal Daniel and I, and to help us escape. And his light was still dim.

My thoughts returned to Daniel. He was somewhere close by. I wondered with a pang in my chest if they would uncover his body so Rescue could take him back to the station. The thought of them putting his mangled body on a stretcher nearly made me lose my mind. But I couldn't go back to the station without him. I'd have to ask Allador...

A few more tears fell at the thought and I tried to stop myself. I needed to pull myself together, but there was a hole in my chest. One that would never be filled. I still needed to get out of here and back to the station. Back to air. I had a headache from the lack of oxygen. So I needed to think. How was I going to even get out of this hole?

Malvolio would be here somewhere too. And the others. I didn't care if they didn't find them. Rescue can find them later. Malvolio could stay buried forever for all I cared.

"He is deceased," Allador informed me.

CHAPTER 53

I Had to See

It was like a knife to the heart. I already knew Daniel was gone, but to hear Allador say it so casually hit me hard. Maybe the Ampari didn't understand grief.

"We have not uncovered the body. He does not deserve it."

My heart kind of twisted. Surely he wasn't talking about Daniel like that. *"Who do you mean? Malvolio?"*

"Yes."

"Good."

Hate welled up inside, threatening to overwhelm me. I wouldn't normally say that when informed of someone's death, but at that moment, I was truly glad that he'd died.

But then I thought, so had Daniel. I'd never had such a hollow ache in my chest before.

I didn't ask Allador about Daniel. I didn't want to hear the words. I couldn't bear hearing him say it. I felt I'd failed him when I'd let go, even though I knew in my heart that I couldn't have held on any longer. But how could I go on living with that guilt? How could I go to sleep each night without him snuggling up next to me?

I tried to stop the tears; I had to get out of here. My brain was screaming for more oxygen and my lungs were burning. My head was throbbing and it was fuzzy again. I couldn't think straight.

I looked around wildly to see if there was some way to climb up to the surface, but it was difficult to see anything beyond the light thrown off by the Ampari. They moved about as if agitated, but I ignored them.

"All others are deceased."

"Oh." I didn't know what else to say. I'd assumed that no one could

have survived, but it still hurt to hear it. Even though Sarinda had tried to kill me, I didn't think she was a bad person — just misguided. She must have really loved Xander.

The shuttle would've left hours ago, judging by how dark the sky was. Damaris was the only person who knew we were down here. Once they detected the collapse, would he tell someone we were in the area? I had no idea.

If I could make my way to the surface, I would at least have a chance of finding the landing site. I assumed there would be people from Katoa coming to assess the damage at some point.

Katoa Labs knew there were people down here and that the device didn't activate. Malvolio and the others would not be answering their Coms, so they would send someone to investigate.

I rubbed my temples, but the only thing that could get rid of this awful headache was oxygen. I took a few deep breaths before standing up, but my knees were jelly and I had to let myself sink to the ground, rather than fall. I looked around again, searching for a section that looked easy to climb. I was in a cleared area, and there were rocks of all shapes and sizes scattered everywhere.

Allador told me the other Ampari had stressed that they would *only* talk to me and Daniel. No other humans. My brain must have been fuzzier than I thought. I thought he'd said they would only talk to me *and* Daniel...

I stood up again, and that's when I saw him.

My blood ran cold. He was lying on his back with his arms spread out by his sides and his clothing was blackened from the laser blasts. So they *had* uncovered him so his body could be taken back.

I didn't want to look.

But I had to look. I had to get to him. I had to hold him one last time. Sharwok's blackened face flashed in my mind. Tears fell freely as I crawled toward him, thinking, *I must be crazy. And really sick.*

My insides were twisted into knots. My heart felt like it was bleeding inside my chest. I still couldn't believe it, even though I knew it was true. How could he be dead?

All the time I spent avoiding him to spare myself this pain and I'd lost him anyway.

The closer I got, the worse I felt. I was going to throw up. I was lightheaded. Breathing was a struggle. What if he was unrecognisable? I stopped for a second, but I *had* to see. I had to keep going.

Why was I doing this? Why did I want to see this? Maybe I needed to confirm it — to get it into my head that he really was gone. I thought if I didn't look, if I just ran out of here, I'd spend the rest of my life wondering if he was still alive and if there was something I could've done...

It became brighter as I neared him and I assumed that Allador or one of the other Ampari had moved closer. I didn't know whether I wanted the extra light. That would mean I would be able to see more gruesome details.

As I came close enough to touch him, I couldn't bring myself to look at his face. I made myself look everywhere else.

I frowned. Besides the blackened shoulders, arms and chest, I couldn't see any damage to his clothing. I expected all of it to be soaked in blood. His limbs looked normal, his knuckles were bloody and, as I dared to finally look at his face, I saw that although there was dirt and blood on his skin here and there, there was no sign of injury.

CHAPTER 54

It's a Long Story

I blinked in disbelief. *"What? How?"*

"The others," Allador said. *"I told you. They helped me."*

Tears filled my eyes and as I leaned forward to take a closer look, they landed on Daniel's chest. *"You mean... Is he...?"* I asked as I scrambled to find a pulse on the side of his throat.

"Yes, he is alive. I thought you knew this."

My heart swelled in my chest and his pulse beat steadily beneath my fingertips. I couldn't believe it.

I'd lost all hope. I'd thought he was gone forever...

What about the laser blasts?

I pulled his clothing away from his neck and shoulders. Nothing. He'd been fully healed too. I choked out a sob.

I reached over and put my arms around his neck and held him tightly. Relief flooded through me. Wrapped around me. Warmed me from the inside out. His heart beat against my ear. It wasn't long before I was sobbing into his shoulder. I couldn't help it. It made breathing so much harder and my headache pounded out a drumbeat inside my skull, but I couldn't stop.

Allador seemed perplexed by my behaviour. I didn't care.

After my sobs had slowed and finally stopped, I stayed there enjoying the feel of him. His skin against mine. The steady rise and fall of his chest. His beating heart...

He needed more air — we both did — but what could I do? None of the air tanks would've survived. Maybe he wouldn't regain consciousness without a more oxygen-rich atmosphere. Panic snaked its way down my spine. I didn't want to think about it too much, but now it was eating at my thoughts.

I looked around. The Ampari were milling about, possibly talking amongst themselves. There was no way I could carry Daniel out of here. If he woke up, we could climb to the surface, but I had no idea when or if that would happen.

If Malvolio hadn't tried to kill Daniel, he wouldn't have brought the ceiling down on us.

It was hard to believe he was gone. I thought about my reaction when Allador told me he was dead. I didn't really want him dead — I was just so angry after all the things he'd done. And I thought he'd killed Daniel.

No more stalker. No more jealous ex-boyfriend. And hopefully, no more training and torture at Katoa Labs. It was like a heavy weight had been lifted from my soul. But I would've preferred that he be locked up as a punishment instead.

I stopped myself. I needed to do something; we had to get out of here.

It was still dark, but, what time did the sun rise on Kronos?

I looked up at Allador. "How long till the sun rises?"

"Soon."

That wasn't helpful.

"I need to get out, up to the surface," I told Allador as I pointed upwards.

The lack of oxygen would make it difficult to climb, but maybe I could lift him using telekinesis.

Why didn't I think of that sooner?

Allador lifted both arms out to the side. *"I help."*

Before I could ask what he meant, I started to float up into the air and I gasped. Allador and Daniel floated with me.

I'd lifted lots of things with my mind, but I'd never been lifted myself. It was a nerve-wracking experience. I tried to calm my racing heart and slow my breathing.

It was about twenty metres straight up; I wouldn't have made it out by climbing, especially with the thin atmosphere.

No wonder we couldn't lift the rocks and dirt by ourselves...

Allador lowered me down first and I turned to watch him place Daniel carefully onto the grass.

I knelt and checked his pulse and breathing again. His pulse was strong, but his breathing still worried me. It was shallow, but I had to keep telling myself that it was because of the lack of oxygen and not because there was something wrong. Allador had healed him. He should have been in perfect health.

So why wasn't he conscious? I leaned over and hugged him again. *Please wake up.*

Allador moved closer to us as the other Ampari appeared above the rim of the hole they'd created. I thanked them all for saving our lives. I would've been thankful if they had only managed to save me, but my life would have been empty without the man I held in my arms right now. As I thought about it, a lone tear escaped.

Now I had to somehow find someone to help us.

I gave a start when I heard noises in the distance. My heart leapt as I saw lights moving toward us.

"Daniel! They're here!" I said aloud. Then I shouted to the approaching humans. "Hey! Over here! We need help!"

Hearing their return shouts was a comfort, but I didn't move from Daniel's side.

The Ampari moved back, and some of them disappeared from sight. *"Don't go!"* I told them. *"They need to see you and know you helped us."*

They stayed and watched as Rescue entered the clearing we were in. The fact that they weren't wearing the security uniforms of Katoa Labs was a relief.

There were looks of shock and surprise on their faces, but I stood and told them not to be afraid. My head spun and I swayed a little, but I managed to stay upright. The last thing I needed was to faint before I could explain the Ampari.

I told Rescue we were in a cavern when it collapsed and made sure they knew that the Ampari had played a big part in saving our lives. My breathing was erratic with the exertion of talking.

All eyes and torches were focused on me and Daniel, which made me nervous.

"You don't have masks on!" one man said incredulously.

"No, we don't," I told them. "The atmosphere is too thin to be without a mask, but it's not toxic like we've been told."

They processed that, then a man stepped forward and offered me a mask and oxygen tank. I gladly took them and put the mask on Daniel's face and sealed it. I noticed the difference in his breathing right away, which helped to calm me.

As I stood and turned to face them again, I was given another mask for myself. I couldn't get it on my face fast enough. The air smelled so sweet and fresh and it made me feel better immediately. My head started to unfog. Several people were speaking at once.

"I'm sorry. What did you say?"

Some of them knelt next to Daniel to check him over.

"I was asking if you are injured," he said as he looked from me to Daniel.

"No. We were badly injured, but the Ampari — the Ghosts — healed us." I waved an arm in their general direction.

He frowned. "But how?"

I lifted my chin. "I don't know, but they can. As I told you, we had a lot of injuries. Daniel had even been shot twice with a laser pistol before the collapse."

He looked fascinated, but right now, all I wanted to do was get out of here.

He frowned. "Who shot him? You?"

I glared at the man. "No! I will explain more later," I told him, "but can you get us out of here?"

"Yes," he agreed. "We need to move — ah — what was his name again?"

"Daniel."

"Yeah, Daniel." He turned to his fellow Rescue workers. "Is the patient able to be moved?"

"Yes, Sir," a female Rescue worker replied with confidence. "There are no injuries. All vitals are stable. He's just unconscious."

He turned back to me. "What's your name?"

"Lennina."

"I'm Taras. Are there any others down here with you?"

I took a deep breath. "There was, down there," I pointed over the edge, "but they didn't survive. They are still buried."

His eyes widened and he motioned for someone to look over the edge. "Who?"

"Malvolio Dermid, Sarinda Markin, and about seven security guards from Katoa Labs."

Taras's eyes widened and others gasped. "Are you sure?"

Two people walked back from the edge and shook their heads.

"Yes," I answered. "There was a fight. It will take too long to explain now. Malvolio shot Daniel with a laser pistol and ended up shooting the roof."

"What?"

"Malvolio was trying to kill us both." I was still weak from going so long without enough oxygen and I swayed again. "It's a long story. I'll tell you everything when we get back to Perseus. Can we please go?"

He put a hand on my elbow to steady me and all I could think of was the fact that there was no jolt of Lightning or buzzing sensation. Crazy, I know, but there you have it.

"Are you okay?"

"Yeah."

He turned to the others. "Okay," he said in a voice loud enough for them all to hear. "Let's book it. Let's get Daniel and Lennina to safety. The recovery team can extract the bodies when they arrive."

They moved like a well-oiled machine, lifting Daniel onto a stretcher and strapping him in. Taras asked if I was okay to walk and I nodded.

We said goodbye to the Ampari and I thanked them again. I promised to contact them soon. Allador told me he would call me, which sounded weird, like he could just call on the Vid. He would probably turn up randomly wherever I happened to be up on the station.

"Let's move," Taras urged when he saw that Daniel was secure.

The trip to the shuttle was uneventful, but Daniel was still unconscious. I'd been so sure that he'd come around once he'd had some oxygen. I tried not to worry.

I was glad it only took a few minutes to get to the shuttle. We were taken aboard, and after the hatch was sealed and the area pressurised, we took off our masks. Daniel's was left on. They'd adjusted it to give him extra oxygen. One of the medics asked how I was feeling and if I needed to put the mask back on, but I felt fine besides the headache, which was fading fast.

They gave me some water to drink. I couldn't remember how long it had been since I'd eaten or had a drink.

We quickly moved from the cargo bay to the main part of the ship. Two of the medics monitored Daniel as he was put into a secure bunk. I sat in a nearby seat and we strapped ourselves in before lifting off.

I couldn't keep my eyes off Daniel. I wanted to hold him in my arms again. I waited impatiently until we'd cleared the planet's atmosphere and we were able to move around.

Before I could get out of my seat, one of the medics asked how I was doing. He introduced himself as Mokalu and checked my pulse and blood pressure.

As I looked at Daniel lying so still in the bunk, I couldn't help but worry.

Please, I thought desperately. *Please wake up. I love you. I need you. I don't know what I would do without you.*

CHAPTER 55
Please Wake Up

I wanted to cry. He was alive, but I felt like I was losing him all over again. I knew it was silly to think that way, but I couldn't help it.

Why wouldn't he wake up?

Mokalu checked Daniel's vitals again and said, "He seems fine. He should come around soon. Maybe even before we get to Perseus."

My breath caught. I stumbled over to the bunk as Mokalu moved away and sat on a nearby seat. I sat on the side of the bunk, wanting to be as close as I could.

It wasn't close enough. I shifted closer and looked down at his face. I wouldn't be able to relax until he woke up.

I leaned down and pressed my forehead against his and closed my eyes. *"Daniel? Please wake up. I need you. I love you..."*

He moved and I jumped back. His eyes opened and I gasped as my heart skipped a beat.

Daniel's eyes rolled around in his head and Mokalu darted forward. "Daniel. I'm Mokalu. You're safe. We are en route to Perseus Station. How are you feeling?"

Daniel frowned at him and blinked a few times. "I... I'm good."

He looked away from Mokalu and his eyes found mine. Tears sprung to my eyes as he smiled at me. "Hey, you."

"Hi." I tried to hold back a sob, but it escaped.

"Hey, don't cry, Cal."

At the mention of my nickname, tears flowed freely and he sat up and wrapped me in his strong arms, bringing a jolt of Lightning and the buzzing sensation. "What happened? How'd we get here? Where's Malvolio?"

To have him holding me after thinking I'd never be in his arms again was kind of heart-wrenching. "Malvolio's dead. So are the others."

"What? How?"

I wished I didn't have to relive it all so soon.

I took a deep breath. "He shot you again. You almost... died. I pushed him as he fired and his hand flew upwards. He blasted the roof and caused it to come crashing down on us." The memory made me shiver.

Daniel held me closer. "How did we survive that?"

"When the roof came down, I held the rocks above you with a shield and Allador held them above me."

"Whoah..."

"But it was so hard and I was already weakened from Sarinda's attack and I couldn't hold out. The other Ampari came to help when we couldn't hold them any longer..." I had to fight back the tears so I could talk. "And... When I woke up... I thought you were..."

I couldn't say any more. Daniel held me tighter and rocked me a little. "Shhh."

I relished the buzzing and just being in his arms.

"Hey. I'm here now. We're alive. That's what matters. It's okay." He tensed. "What happened to the Ampari?"

"They're all okay. We saved them. Then they moved half a mountain to save us and healed all our injuries."

I sensed his relief. "That's great. That's fantastic. We'll help them stop the mining."

I smiled. The Rescue workers probably thought we were a bit crazy. I heard voices around us, but didn't even try to understand what they were saying.

I pulled away so I could see Daniel's face. His eyes were wet with tears. I noticed him looking at the trails of blood on my face. I must have looked like death warmed up.

My heart skipped a beat as he took off his mask, then leaned forward and kissed me. I melted into him and returned the kiss eagerly. The universe faded away into the background and there was just him. His kiss was fevered and hungry and I scrunched up his overalls in one hand and tangled my fingers in his hair with the other. I pulled him closer. I couldn't get close enough.

Daniel pulled away from me with a questioning look.

"Are you sure you're okay?" he asked as we both caught our breath.

"Yes. I'm more than okay now that you're here with me."

He smiled and kissed me again like there'd been no interruption. That was fine with me. My body flushed with heat. My mind raced along with my heart. There was so much love for him surging through me. This is what I thought I'd never have again. This was everything I'd ever wanted. To be here with him. I'd never felt so happy. I wanted to stay here forever and forget about the world and about the trouble we'd be in. There'd be a million questions to answer about Malvolio and the Ampari and Katoa Labs and the atmosphere on Kronos, but none of that mattered right now. All that mattered was him.

"I love you so much," he said.

The thought kind of filled my mind and body. I breathed deeply, taking in every bit of him. His smell and the feel of his lips against mine. His hair and his face and his hard muscles under his clothing. His hands that were roaming over me. I belonged in his arms.

"I love you too," I told him. I made sure the thought and all my feelings filled him up too.

Somewhere far away, I heard someone say, "Get a room."

That made me laugh against Daniel's mouth and he chuckled. I pulled back a little.

Without taking my eyes off Daniel, I said, "We will."

EPILOGUE
This is For You

Daniel manoeuvred the hovercar into the driveway of my house on Azaeli and I couldn't wait to race inside and hug my family.

We'd endured the intense investigation of Katoa and had told them everything. We didn't hold anything back.

The results of the investigation were shocking. Katoa had only employed people with the DNA marker that was linked to the Lightning ability so they could study them and try to trigger their Talent and Lightning Connections. The miners were exposed to the raw Amakio by the very nature of their jobs, but the other workers on the space station weren't, so Katoa had deliberately exposed them without their knowledge.

Once their Talent manifested, Katoa Labs would take over and put the people through their training program, hoping to create soldiers with specialised skills. Not all of the people had developed Talent, and some didn't form a Lightning Connection, but there were enough of them that had done both.

Katoa was determined to be the only company producing — and profiting from — these soldiers, but we'd busted their operation wide open, as well as saved the Ampari from total annihilation.

Then there was their plan to terraform the planet. They were in deep trouble.

The front door slid open as I stepped out of the car and I was engulfed in a group hug full of laughter and tears.

Once we'd broken apart, I introduced Mum and Adamo to Daniel and Mum gave him a big hug before we went inside.

I walked along next to Adamo and had to look up to see his face. "I can't believe how tall you are. You've grown since I was last here."

He grinned and rubbed the top of my head. "Yep. You're an even shorter shorty now."

"Yeah, well, you're still my little brother."

We'd already told them about everything that had happened through a number of Vid calls, so we didn't have to sit down and relive it all. I was glad because we needed to put it behind us and get on with our lives. We needed to choose a career path that suited our new abilities, but there were still some doctors and scientists that wanted to study us further. As long as they didn't treat us the way the doctors at Katoa Labs did, I was okay with them running some tests every now and then.

Mum went into the kitchen as we settled down at the dining room table and came back with some hot drinks. "Welcome to the family, Daniel."

"Thank you, Mrs Callista."

"Please, call me Myesha."

Mum didn't waste any time. "Have you guys decided what you're going to do career-wise and have you decided where you're going to live?"

I nodded. "We're staying here — if that's okay with you?"

She smiled. "Yes, of course."

"And we're still looking into career options for the Talented. The main problem is the Lightning ability. People don't know what it is, and if they do, they don't know what to do with it."

She rubbed the back of her hand. "Yes. It would be a problem."

I was so happy that Daniel had agreed to move here. I would have moved anywhere to be with him, but he understood that I needed my family right now.

We spent the afternoon together talking and laughing and it was like Daniel had been part of the family all along.

I needed this.

After dinner, Mum and Adamo went into the kitchen to clean up and Daniel and I snuggled up on the lounge chair.

Daniel reached into his pocket and pulled out a small metal box. "This is for you."

My heart leapt. "What is it?"

"You'll see."

I tried to open it, but the latch wouldn't budge; it had been welded shut. I turned it over a few times and tried again, but had to give up.

I held it out to him. "Can you help me? It won't open."

He smiled at me. "Well, you see, that's the point."

"I don't follow."

"Now no one can put your heart in a box ever again."

I remembered the conversation where I'd said that it felt like Malvolio had locked my heart away in a box and my heart melted. Daniel was so thoughtful and so perfect.

Tears ran down my cheeks as I wrapped my arms around him. "I love you, Daniel Javolo!"

———— ★·☆·★ ————

This is the end of this story, but not the end of this book. Keep reading for some extra goodies:

A bonus scene

An excerpt from the first book in the *Tamisan Series*, **TAMISAN**

An offer of a free book

Acknowledgements

A list of other books by Susan McKenzie

About the author

———— ★·☆·★ ————

Did you enjoy this book?

Help the next reader to enjoy it too.

Reviews are such a fantastic way for people to express the way a book made them feel. A way to share it with the world.

Indie authors don't have the huge budgets that the big New York publishers have, but we have something more powerful. We have loyal readers like you.

It would be so awesome if you could share what you thought of this book by leaving a review on the site where you purchased it.

Thank you so much.

Sue

——— ⋆·☆·⋆ ———

Keep reading for a bonus scene of Lennina's first day working with Daniel Javolo

——— ⋆·☆·⋆ ———

Bonus scene
First Day Working with Javolo

I took a deep breath to calm my nerves. This was not a big deal. I didn't even know why I was worrying about it.

I hadn't even been this nervous on my first day working here. Maybe somewhere deep down I felt somehow responsible for what had happened to Rogan, although I wasn't even at work when he'd lost his mind.

I entered my login details and waited for the Nav Computer to load the Navigational program.

Rogan had claimed he saw lights in the tunnels, and from what I'd been told, that was a sure sign he'd been down there too long. Everyone knew it. Working underground for long periods of time could take their toll on some people.

There were others, of course, that had worked for Katoa for years without any problems, so I guessed you had to have the right mindset for that kind of work.

Me? I knew I couldn't work underground. The thought made me feel ill.

Information was displayed on my screen about the planet and the locations of Amakio deposits.

The weird thing was, Rogan hadn't shown any of the signs we were told to look for. The day before yesterday, he'd been fine. We got through our day without anything unusual happening and he'd always been calm and level-headed, even when we'd had some ground movement down on the planet we were mining.

When I'd arrived at work this morning, my supervisor, Mr Sonrisa, had pulled me aside and told me I had been assigned a new partner. Just like that.

My new Digger showed up as a four-digit number on my screen.
6896.

That was it. It was so impersonal. We were all just numbers to a huge mining company like Katoa Intergalactic Mining and Exploration and the Diggers were on the bottom of the pile.

"Good morning," I paused and checked the info I'd been given, "Daniel Javolo."

His voice came through, scratchy and off-frequency. "Good morning. I'm sorry. I don't have my paperwork here in my Mech-suit so I can't remember your name."

Why were my hands trembling?

"It's Lennina Callista. How are you this morning?"

"Very well, thank you. Sorry again about your name."

I smiled. "That's quite alright. I had to check my paperwork to remember yours."

He chuckled.

I took a deep breath. "Okay. Let's start on the safety checks."

"Copy that."

We ran through all the routine checks to make sure the Mech-suit and all its digging equipment was functioning correctly, then went through tests on the sensors that helped us pinpoint the mineral deposits under the ground. They correlated data gathered from sixteen orbiting satellites, as well as the Mech-suits worn by the other Diggers.

Once that was done and the last of the data came through on the location of a deposit, we were ready to go.

"Enter the tunnels and proceed through the northern tunnel for one hundred metres."

"Copy that."

I fidgeted with the edge of my sleeve as I waited for Javolo to walk the one hundred metres. This part of the job was boring. All sorts of things flew through my mind, but I couldn't talk about any of them. We had to stick to relevant communication.

My stomach fluttered and I was too hot.

I'd tried to strike up small conversations with Rogan, but he'd shut me down or ignored me. We weren't supposed to be talking about anything other than work.

I was honestly thinking about severing my contract with The Company and going home. This wasn't the life for me. I'd always been a bit of a loner, but sitting here day after day and not being able to talk freely was getting to me.

This job was supposed to eventually lead to a better position in Research and Development, but the contract for this position was for two years. I'd only been here a few weeks and it wasn't getting any better.

Could I put up with this meaningless job until I could do something useful for the company? I had some ideas for how they could use better materials for their masks and the Mech-suits, but no one here seemed to be interested in any of my suggestions so far. I was obviously pitching my ideas to the wrong people and would have to wait for my chance to speak to the people in R and D. They would be interested, surely. Who wouldn't want to improve their technology and efficiency and save money in the long run?

I took a couple of deep breaths to calm my nerves.

"I'm at the destination. Which way should I turn?"

I looked at his location on my screen. 6896. I tapped the number and changed the setting so it displayed Javolo's surname instead. He was a person. Not just a number.

"Turn to your left. Walk forward for twenty metres and you should arrive at another intersection. Turn right."

"Copy that."

Silence again. I'd only just started working with Javolo, but so far, all I could think of was telling Sonrisa I quit.

I needed to stop thinking like that. It hadn't even been a full hour. Give the guy a go.

But it wasn't actually the person. It was the fact that we had to be so formal and stuffy and only speak when we needed to. That's what was driving me crazy.

My fingers tapped out a rhythm on the desk. Maybe if I had some music to listen to, I could get through my days with my sanity intact.

I'd already asked about having some music playing quietly while I worked. I'd received a firm "No" because there was a lot of interference coming from the planet, causing havoc with all their equipment and having music playing over the air would make it almost impossible to hear each other.

I tapped out the beat to one of my favourite songs to amuse myself.

"What's that noise?"

I pulled my hands away. "Oh, sorry. That was me. I was tapping my fingers on the desk. It's just that it's so quiet and they won't let me have any music and— Sorry. I'm raving on a bit."

"No. It's okay. Continue to rave. I find it too quiet too. I've tried to get them to pipe music into my Mech-suit, but they won't do it."

It was funny that we'd both requested the same thing for the same reason.

"I think I'm going stir crazy."

He chuckled. "I'm already crazy. I guess we'll have to fill the silence some other way."

"How?"

"With a decent conversation."

I sighed. "That would be nice."

"Now, where to?"

I directed him through a few more tunnels before he arrived at the area we were looking for. "Go down from the corner about five metres and there should be the start of a vein to your right."

There was a pause. "Yup. Spot on. I'll get this stuff out in no time."

He powered up the rock-breaker on his Mech-suit and started digging.

We couldn't speak while he worked, but I didn't mind this time. Why did it annoy me so much a couple of minutes ago, but not now?

I found myself waiting eagerly to find out what we'd talk about. Maybe it wouldn't be so boring in this dull little room all by myself.

And at least we had one thing in common; we both liked music.

The noise stopped. "All done."

"That was quick."

"Yeah, well, I figured if I hurried, we could get back to what we were talking about. So, what kind of music do you like?"

Wow. Javolo was so different to Rogan. I only hesitated a few seconds before telling him I liked a wide variety of music and that I played keyboard. His musical tastes were very similar and he liked to play drums.

He hadn't heard of any of the performers I liked — and vice versa — but seeing how we were probably from different planets, it made sense.

"Where are you from?" I asked.

"Taon. In the Kharas System."

I smiled. "I'm from Azaeli. It's in the same System, so we're neighbours."

He chuckled. "Yes. We are."

I giggled.

Neighbours.

Our home planets were millions of kilometres apart.

"Okay. I've filled my tub. Tell me where to go."

That comment could be taken the wrong way, but I didn't bite. I gave him directions to get back to the shuttle and we talked about our home planets on the way.

He emptied the floating tub and was set to head back down underground. "Hey, Cal. Can you get me back to the spot so we can get this show on the road? I reckon one more load and I'll need to dig again."

"Cal?"

"Yeah. I don't know — it kinda suits you."

Warmth spread across my chest. No one had ever thought to shorten my surname before. It was sort of cute.

I smiled. I liked Javolo. Maybe I'd stay on at Katoa for a while longer and see how things panned out.

—— ★·☆·★ ——

Keep reading for an excerpt from the first book in the *Tamisan Series,*
TAMISAN

EXCERPT: TAMISAN (TAMISAN BOOK 1)

Chapter 1

I felt a strange apprehension when I stepped out of the shuttle into the sunlight and it sent a shiver down my spine, but the feeling quickly subsided as I looked around me. This place was magnificent! It was a tropical jungle paradise.

Tall trees surrounded us on all sides. The only break in the canopy big enough to let in the sunlight properly was the clearing where our small shuttle, the Outrider, had landed for emergency repairs.

It was so wild and free and different to the world I knew. I'd grown up in a city on Earth, which was so ordered and sterile and 'civilised.'

Craning my neck, I turned in a circle. All around us were huge tree trunks with vines that intertwined around them and through the branches of smaller trees and shrubs, slowly choking them to death while reaching ever upward to the sun. There were ferns that spread their fronds several metres in all directions and fungi in various shades of orange, red and yellow. The scents and smells of a hundred different flowers, plants and animals were concentrated in the thick, humid air.

The other five passengers around me were awed by Althar 3's beauty too, and they stood open-mouthed in the clearing. I stifled a laugh. We looked ridiculous.

We'd travelled across the universe to start work with the Voyager Division to study and observe the natives on this super-primitive planet, but the shuttle taking us from the main ship to the surface had developed engine trouble, forcing us to land in the middle of the dense jungle.

This wasn't part of the plan, but it was a great diversion. We had been headed to Station Jannali, a hidden underground base somewhere in this jungle, and now we were getting an up-close-and-personal look at the local scenery.

I could see that the shuttle pilot had already started working on the engine.

As soon as Station Jannali had heard we had to land, they'd located a suitable spot and given us orders to collect some plant and soil samples so we could make ourselves useful. They gave us a list of the kinds of plants they wanted, so we took some sampling equipment and a PocketPC that contained the pictures they'd sent of what was required. We spread out, wandering amongst the vines and blooms at the edge of the clearing.

I didn't start work straight away. My mind was trying to process everything I was seeing. It was so surreal. We'd been briefed on the flora and fauna on Althar and what to expect, including the kind of wildlife that lurked in the jungle, and it was actually full of very large and very dangerous creatures that basically belonged in the Jurassic or Cretaceous Period of Earth's distant past. They were so similar it was kind of unnerving.

Another shiver travelled the length of my spine at the thought. What if one of those dinosaur look-alikes was nearby right now? Why did Jannali give permission for us to wander around out here without any training or weapons for protection? What kind of company had I signed up with?

I started to think that maybe I'd made a huge mistake. I was a new graduate from the Academy. I was qualified to deal with *computer*-related problems. I had so many options open to me, but I chose to go to the edge of the Known Universe. *I must be crazy.*

What was I doing here? Why did I apply for a job way out here? Was my life at the Academy *that* boring that I jumped at the first opportunity to go off-planet?

My mind answered immediately. *Yes.*

That realisation had my mind reeling. I'd been prepared to leave everything and everyone I'd ever known. That was kind of scary.

Part of our work would involve studying the family units, which would be weird – and also very intriguing – for some members of our group because we didn't have families. The people from Earth were cloned and raised in groups according to age and gender.

I'd learned about the family units that still existed in some of the older cultures on Earth and on other planets. And there were some people on Earth who were against cloning.

A sound like something flapping around in the breeze, followed by an ear-splitting screech, pulled me from my thoughts and I turned to see a large leather-winged reptile flapping its wings madly as it made its way across the clearing, bringing screams from the other female crew members, Larissa and Bazeelia. Even Janssen and Lanu gave a shout as the creature flew past.

Bazeelia was a tall Ziflarian with long, black curly hair that she kept tied up in a high ponytail. She scowled at Janssen and Lanu for laughing at her. "Don't be laughin' at me. That thing was a monster! And it scared *you* too!"

Janssen turned to her, his long white-blonde hair almost blindingly bright in the sunshine. "Hey. Take it easy. We're just messin' with ya."

Lanu got up awkwardly from the spot where he was kneeling in the dirt and stalked over to them. "You've got to admit it was amazing though."

Bazeelia stared at him open-mouthed. "*Amazing?* No. It wasn't. It was *terrifying*!"

Lanu smiled, a look of awe on his face. "But that thing is so similar to the Pteranodon from Earth's past and it flew within a few *metres* of us. It's like going back to the Cretaceous Period and getting a first-hand look."

"Well, you can go look at it and admire its beauty if you want. Pat it. Study it. Although I'm not sure being a Sociologist will help when it comes to dinosaurs. Me? I'm glad I'll be working indoors once we get to Jannali." She flipped her long hair over her shoulder and went back to work.

"Miss Rhodarma?" I jumped. Once I realised who had called me, I cringed inwardly. Kami Olion, the other Sociologist in the group, was standing at the hatch of the shuttle. He was nothing like Lanu. He was a prickly, annoying person. "I heard screams. What has happened?"

If you hadn't refused to come out here, you'd already know.

He'd said the engine trouble was a bad omen. I'd ignored him. I didn't believe in superstitions and had jumped at the chance to see the jungle first-hand.

And what was with the 'Miss Rhodarma'? Did he have to be so formal?

"Please call me Zhenna," I said.

He inclined his head. "Very well."

I gave him a small smile, feeling awkward. "Everything's okay. It was just a flying reptile. It flew through the clearing and gave us a fright."

He shook his head. "Going outside was a bad idea. I said it was a bad idea. But would anyone listen? No, they didn't. Will you come inside, please, where it's safe? The others won't listen. And I have a *bad* feeling." He drew out the word "bad," like that would make me believe him.

I frowned. Why was he only asking me? "Umm, I can't. Jannali wants the samples. It's going to give a bad impression if we refuse."

His eyebrows drew together and his mouth turned down at the corners. He turned on his heel and went back inside.

I sighed, relieved he was gone. He'd been a pain in everyone's butt on the journey out here. He must have been really good at his job because I was sure he didn't get hired for his personality.

"Don't worry about him," Larissa said as she walked up to me, her long white-blonde hair as blinding as Janssen's. "He's just a superstitious old grump."

I laughed, then cringed. I hoped he couldn't hear her.

She noticed my reaction. "I don't care if he hears me."

I giggled.

We'd met on the trip out here to The Fringe, as some called it, and became friends right away. It had taken us two weeks at Warp Delta and there wasn't a lot to do aboard the Acronis. We both had an interest in art and liked similar types of music and had spent a lot of time together.

I turned my attention away from the spot where Kami had stood. I needed to actually do the job I was sent out here to do. We headed a bit further into the jungle. I was looking for an orange flower and Larissa was after a type of fungi, which should've been easier for her since she was a Botanist.

As we searched, I saw Larissa stealing glances at Janssen. This wasn't the first time I'd seen her watching him. I was sure she had a crush. She'd shown an interest during the trip out here, but she always insisted that she didn't like him all that much. I smiled.

The next time she looked at me I said, "I saw you looking at him."

—— ★·☆·★ ——

TAMISAN *(Tamisan Book 1)* is available right now. Use the QR Code to grab your copy!

Or type this into your browser: https://books2read.com/tamisan

—— ★·☆·★ ——

Keep reading for a chance to sign up for a free novelette, **THE ALIEN**

YOUR FREE BOOK IS WAITING

The novelette

THE ALIEN

is free for a limited time. You just need to tell me where
to send it

When Lilliana crash-lands her spaceship on a Primitive
planet, she'll have to rely on help from an attractive
local to survive.

**Use the QR Code to follow the link, then enter your name and
email address to get your free book delivered to your inbox**

Or type this link into your browser: https://www.sub-
scribepage.com/thealien

ACKNOWLEDGEMENTS

Up until recently, I've always worked alone when writing. Sure, I've had the support of family and friends, but now I have a group of authors that understand what it's like and help me along my journey. I'd like to thank them personally. They are the 10K Readers + SPF – Sydney Meet Up group. I don't know where I'd be without you all.

I've also gathered a small group of beta readers and I'm so thankful for their help.

And of course, I'd like to thank all of the members of the Sydney Shadows Club who have supported me. I am honoured to be a member of the club.

To my family and friends, a big thank you. Love you all.

Lastly, to Pete, for sharing your life with me. I love you.

Books by Susan McKenzie

THE JADORI SERIES (ONGOING SERIES):

<u>Fire and Magic</u> is being released in a serialized format (1 chapter per week) on <u>reamstories.com</u> right now!

———— ⋆·☆·⋆ ————

THE TAMISAN SERIES (COMPLETED SERIES):

<u>Tamisan</u>
<u>Enigma</u>

———— ⋆·☆·⋆ ————

<u>A Tamisan Novella – Shakiran: Larissa's Story</u>

THE LIGHTNING TOUCH SERIES (COMPLETED SERIES):

<u>Touch of Lightning</u>
<u>Power of Lightning</u>

———— ⋆·☆·⋆ ————

* Just remember, a completed series means you can binge read the whole series now.

———— ⋆·☆·⋆ ————

About the Author

Susan McKenzie is an Australian author who loves creating worlds of fantasy and science fiction with fascinating characters and slow-burn low-spice romance.

Her books are full of interesting and relatable characters who use their psychic abilities or magical powers to fight their way out of trouble.

She loves stories that hit you in the feels.

She's not a typical author coffee addict - but chocolate? Now that's a different story. When she's not writing, she loves to paint, draw, sing, and play the guitar.

Get in touch with Sue.
ReamStories subscription:
https://reamstories.com/susanmckenzie
Amazon author page:
https://www.amazon.com/author/susancarter
Visit Sue's website:
http://susanmckenzieauthor.com
Follow Sue on Facebook:
https://www.facebook.com/SueMcKenzieAuthor

www.ingramcontent.com/pod-product-compliance
Lightning Source LLC
Chambersburg PA
CBHW020133120726
47903CB00007B/2231